Panic on Gull Island

"Frank!" Joe exclaimed.

Frank turned to see why Joe had screamed. Vicious Dobermans, their fangs bared, were tearing across the lawn. The dog in the lead, a huge black and brown beast, bore down rapidly, heading straight for Frank!

"Run!" Joe yelled. He sprinted toward the beach, hoping his brother would follow his lead.

Frank put on a burst of speed, trying to distance himself from the ferocious animals. But the dogs were already snapping at his heels. Frank knew he and Joe had only one chance to escape.

"Get ready!" Frank called as the brothers neared the wall separating Vollrath's property from the beach. "We'll have to jump for it!"

The Hardy Boys Mystery Stories

Available from MINSTREL Books

107

The
HARDY BOYS®

PANIC ON GULL ISLAND

FRANKLIN W. DIXON

A MINSTREL® BOOK

PUBLISHED BY POCKET BOOKS

New York   London   Toronto   Sydney   Tokyo   Singapore

A MINSTREL PAPERBACK *ORIGINAL*

 A Minstrel Book published by
POCKET BOOKS, a division of Simon & Schuster
1230 Avenue of the Americas, New York, NY 10020

Copyright © 1991 by Simon & Schuster
Cover art copyright © 1991 by Paul Bachem
Produced by Mega-Books of New York, Inc.

ISBN: 0-671-69276-3

First Minstrel Books printing April 1991

10 9 8 7 6 5 4 3 2

Contents

PANIC ON
GULL ISLAND

A.J. Wessler

1 Trouble in the Air

"Iola's missing!" Chet Morton gasped as he ran up the driveway to the Hardy home. Seventeen-year-old Joe Hardy, behind the wheel of the Hardy brothers' van, immediately hit the brakes and signaled for Chet to jump in.

"My sister's disappeared!" Chet repeated breathlessly as he hoisted himself into the passenger seat. "They said she was on her way to the beach, but she never got there."

"Slow down, Chet," Joe urged his friend. He tried to appear calm, but he knew if anything had happened to Iola Morton, it would affect him as much as Chet. Joe and Iola had been going together for a long time, often accompanying Joe's older brother, Frank, and his girlfriend, Callie Shaw.

1

"But I just talked to her two days ago," Joe said, running his hand through his blond hair.

"We've got to do something!" Chet exclaimed.

"I know, Chet," Joe responded, fighting to control his emotions. "We will. But the first thing we have to do is pick up Dad and Frank at the airport."

Joe backed the van onto High Street, shifted gears, then took the shortest route out of Bayport's residential area to the airport expressway.

"Iola hasn't been seen or heard from for over a day now," Chet continued. "As you know, she's on spring break with her friend Daphne. They're staying on Gull Island, off the coast of Florida. Anyway, Iola left the motel to join Daphne out at the beach yesterday morning, but she never got there. The police found her car abandoned on a side road."

"Is Daphne all right?"

"She's fine," answered Chet.

"Was it the police who called you?"

"No, Daphne's uncle Regis Garnett phoned. He runs the Royal Palms, the old resort motel on Gull Island that they're staying at."

"Are the police working on it?"

"Not really," Chet sputtered, frustration in his voice. "Mr. Garnett said there's one officer for the entire island, and thinks Iola took off to find a better beach somewhere."

"Right," Joe said scornfully, "like Iola would just leave her car and take off."

"I'm afraid something terrible has happened," Chet said quietly.

2

"Has there been a ransom call or a note?"

"Nothing," Chet replied. "They just found her car. But if you ask me, I think the police officer's wrong and Iola was kidnapped. We have to find her."

"Don't worry. As soon as we pick up Dad and Frank," Joe announced, grim determination in his voice, "we're leaving for Florida."

Chet sighed with relief. "I was hoping you'd say that."

In the short time since leaving the Hardy home, Joe had paid little attention as the skies clouded over. Now he noticed that a storm had moved in across Barmet Bay. Heavy rain began pelting the van. Even with the windshield wipers switched to high, Joe had trouble seeing the road.

In spite of the storm Joe deftly steered the van into the lane leading to Bayport International Airport. A few moments later they pulled out of the rain and into a space on the second floor of the parking garage.

"Let's hurry," Joe said. "Frank's been helping Dad on a big case, but I want to tell them about Iola before they give me an update."

Fenton Hardy, the internationally famous private detective, had called from Chicago early that morning to tell his son that he and Frank would be arriving on flight 906, due in at 1:38 P.M. Joe could tell by his father's voice that the case against a gang of smugglers was not going well.

"Is that the case you were talking to the guy at the phone company about?" Chet asked as the two

3

approached a sign with an arrow directing them to the main concourse.

Joe braced himself against the strong winds and gusts of rain that whipped through the unprotected garage. He and Chet pulled their jacket collars up and hurried through the automatic doors.

"Yes. Dad's been helping out the government," Joe explained. "Somebody's stealing massive supplies of replacement parts for foreign products, especially anything electronic. Then they resell the parts to dealers and service centers at exorbitant prices."

"So that's why it took so long to find a dealer who could install a new recording head on my VCR," Chet said. "It would have been cheaper to buy a new recorder."

"It's even worse with auto parts," Joe continued. "They're so expensive and hard to find as it is. This gang has somehow cornered the market on foreign supplies for the East Coast, and if we can't find out who's behind it fast, they may soon have the whole country in their grasp."

Joe quickened his step, and Chet nearly had to run to keep up. "Anyway, Dad gave me some phone numbers to trace from an office in Chicago he thinks the gang is using as their front. My friend at the phone company told me there have been over a hundred calls from that office to a business called Warehouse Systems, Inc., down in Miami, Florida, owned by a guy named George Kulp. I wasn't able to get any particular name on the Chicago end, but that's something Dad can look into."

Joe led the way over to the escalator. The boys bounded down several steps at a time. Upon reaching the boarding level, Joe hurried ahead to the airline's counter to check the latest time on the Hardys' flight. According to the monitor, the plane was due to arrive at gate B-5, but not at its scheduled time. The word *Delayed* flashed beside the flight number.

"It's this weather," the attendant at the counter, a friendly, neatly uniformed woman in her twenties, explained in response to the look on Joe's face. "There's a major storm system along the entire East Coast. Our radar's down temporarily, and the tower reports the winds are too heavy to permit landing. It shouldn't be very long, though," she added with a forced smile.

"As long as we have some time to kill," Chet said, heading toward the snack bar next to a newsstand, "let's get something to eat."

Joe followed his hefty friend and ordered a small cola, then sat down at a table next to the window. He shook his head in disbelief as the server piled Chet's tray with two hamburgers, a large order of fries, two cans of soda, and a hot apple turnover. "How can you eat all that at a time like this?" Joe asked.

Chet sat down across the table from Joe. "You know I always eat when I'm worried," he said.

Joe would normally have made a comment about his friend's tendency to overeat or his large size, but Joe wasn't in the mood for conversation. He just stared at the rain that was sheeting down the window. The panoramic view of the runways was completely distorted.

"You never know how long we might be here," Chet mumbled with his mouth full. "You sure you don't want anything to eat?"

Joe shook his head and continued staring out the window.

An hour had passed, Joe noted by glancing at the airport clock, and there was still no indication that flight 906 was going to land.

"I know there hasn't been any announcement," Joe commented, "but it sure looks like the airport is closed down." Suddenly thunder cracked in the distance. The storm was getting worse.

"I wonder how long a plane can circle before it runs out of fuel?" Chet asked.

"I've been asking myself the same thing," Joe said anxiously. "Maybe they routed the plane to another airport. I'll go check."

While Chet made a second trip to the snack bar, Joe headed for the airline ticket counter and saw that the woman attendant who had originally told him the flight was delayed had been joined by another uniformed employee, this one a gray-haired man. The two began speaking in hushed tones. Sensing trouble, Joe tried to look like anyone else standing around, but he edged closer and concentrated on their whispered conversation. The man was clearly nervous. Joe couldn't pick up everything, but what he did hear sent a chill down his spine.

"No choice," the man was saying. "He said

6

they've got to come in now." An announcement on the PA drowned out several words, then Joe heard, ". . . less than two minutes left."

"Is there a problem with flight nine-oh-six?" Joe interrupted the two airline employees.

The woman hesitated. "The good news," she said, her voice quivering as she forced a smile, "is they should be landing any minute."

"And the bad news?" Joe challenged.

The woman looked away.

"Our radar is still down." The man sighed. "The tower's diverted everything else to another airport, but nine-oh-six is too low on fuel. He's got to land now"—the man paused, lowering his eyes—"but the wind on those runways is up to seventy miles an hour."

"The pilot has a lot of experience," the ticket agent said, trying to reassure Joe. "You have friends on the flight?"

"My father and brother."

"They'll be fine, I know it," the woman said.

The phone behind the counter rang, causing all three of them to jump. The woman looked at it as if it would bite her, then grabbed the receiver.

"That was the tower," she reported, hanging up. "They've started their descent."

Upon hearing this, Joe headed quickly back to gate B-5. Chet was sitting in one of the lounge's bright red chairs, finishing the last of his chips.

"Their plane's almost out of fuel," Joe said tersely. Chet was up in an instant, following Joe over to the tall plate-glass window.

7

Joe looked out and saw why the attendants were so worried. The storm was getting worse. The strong winds whipped rain against the glass and sent sheets of water sliding across the glistening runway. Off to the northwest, at some distance, Joe pointed at two faint lights. They were hard to follow, bobbing up and down, sometimes violently left and right. But as he watched them, they grew in intensity. He knew it was flight 906.

"I feel so helpless," Joe said.

"I know," Chet agreed. "For whatever good it'll do, I've got my fingers crossed."

Joe heard the sirens before he spotted them. On the wet tarmac below, several fire trucks raced away from the boarding area toward the runway. Floodlights were switched on. The emergency crews were preparing for the worst.

This is really happening! Joe thought, and felt the hollow sensation of fear. He knew by the silence in the waiting area that word of flight 906's precarious situation had spread. People with worried faces lined up along the window on both sides of Joe.

Emergency vehicles were still pulling into position as the jetliner suddenly appeared out of the cloud cover beyond the airport. Joe could see that the landing gear was down and that the plane was trying to pull up its nose.

"The wind's tossing that plane like a kite," Chet said in awe.

His face pressed against the glass, Joe stared out into the heavy gray skies. Again the aircraft fought to level itself. The nose tilted up but not enough. A wind gust caught flight 906 under its wings, lifting it for an instant, then flinging the huge airliner toward the concrete as if it were a plastic model.

Joe sucked in his breath.

"I can't watch," Chet groaned, covering his eyes.

"They touched down!" shouted Joe.

Joe felt his muscles tense and contract. His right foot pressed reflexively against the floor, as if he could brake the plane to a stop.

"He's losing it!" Joe cried out. Joe could see the tires never got a grip on the ground. The plane began sliding out of control, veering toward the edge of the runway.

"Joe, they're going to hit those planes!" Chet exclaimed, peeking between his fingers at several grounded airliners parked in front of an adjacent concourse.

Joe knew the parked airliners were fueled and ready to go, waiting only for the weather to clear. If 906 collided with one of those planes, only one thing could result—a deadly fireball of destruction.

In an instant he realized that his worst nightmare was coming true as the landing gear of flight 906 collapsed. The plane dropped onto its belly and slid sideways in a shower of sparks and debris past the concourse where Joe was watching in horror. The crippled airliner was only seconds away from slamming into a fully loaded jumbo jet.

2 Hazardous Road

Joe sprang into action. He raced through the boarding ramp's open door, past a startled attendant.

"Hey!" shouted the man. "You can't—"

Joe ignored the attendant and kept on running. His shirt and jacket were already soaked, and he was still under cover.

Fearing the worst, what he saw instead was flight 906 bumping into a landing light. The jolt was enough to deflect the plane. It missed the jet by inches. The crippled airliner finally came to rest in the strip between the main runway and a row of hangars.

Chet Morton pushed past the angry attendant and joined Joe outside. "What do we do now?"

Joe looked around and saw a flight of stairs leading to the tarmac below. "Come on," he called as he started running.

The two boys bounded down the steps two at a time and ran toward the downed airliner.

Joe looked around and surveyed the damage. The mangled wheels and pieces of the plane's aluminum belly lay scattered about the soaked turf.

Smoke rose from the stilled engines. What if a ruptured tank was leaking fuel? Joe thought as he ran faster. If it reaches those hot engines . . .

The maddening drone of rain was broken by fire engines and emergency squads as they converged on the injured aircraft.

The boarding hatch at the front of the plane opened suddenly. Joe saw several bright yellow inflatable emergency slides pop out from the compartments beneath the airliner's doors. Moments later the passengers began sliding to safety one at a time.

Joe hurried over to the nearest slide and began helping people to their feet.

"Are you all right?" he asked each person. Even the ones who insisted they were not hurt looked stunned.

"Do you see Dad or Frank?" Joe shouted above the noise at Chet, who was at another slide assisting passengers.

"Joe!" It was a familiar voice. Joe looked up to see his father standing in the plane's doorway. Fenton and Frank Hardy were assisting a flight attendant. Her uniform sleeve was torn, and she was holding her arm. But, Joe noted happily, his father and brother looked unhurt.

"We need a stretcher over here!" Frank shouted.

11

Joe signaled the driver of an emergency truck with a cherry picker to move into position. As soon as the paramedics had the grimacing attendant lowered to the ground, Joe helped her into the back of an ambulance.

"Are you two okay?" Joe called to his father and brother as they slid down the chute.

"That flight," Frank told his brother with a straight face, "was a little rough." This remark broke the tension, and relieved hugs were exchanged all around. "But," Frank continued, looking right at Chet, "the meal was great!"

When the Hardys and Chet determined that the airport authority's emergency crews had everything under control, the group, with luggage in tow, headed for the van.

Joe took the wheel. As he approached the parking garage's exit ramp, a small 4×4 truck blew its horn insistently and cut in front of the Hardys.

"Hey!" Joe shouted, but the black-and-silver truck was already down and around the exit ramp.

"Just what we need," Frank commented. "Survive a plane crash so we can get into a car accident in a parking garage."

Joe wanted to catch up with the guy, maybe give him a brief lecture on driving etiquette, but there had already been enough excitement for one day.

While he drove, Joe related the news of Iola's disappearance.

"Something's wrong down there," Fenton Hardy said firmly, "and it's up to you boys to find Iola. Drop me off at home," he told them. "If you drive straight through, you should make it to Gull Island in a little over twenty-four hours."

Turning to Chet, Frank said, "Do you want to stop by your house to pick up some things?"

"Sure. It'll only take a minute," he answered.

That decided, Joe next told his father about the calls from several of the gang's Chicago phones to the Miami warehouse owned by George Kulp.

"Good work," Fenton Hardy told Joe.

This was not the first time Fenton had congratulated one of his sons for helping him in his detective work. Both Frank and Joe had given invaluable assistance during many cases. More than that, they had established their own reputation as detectives.

"That gives us a name to go on," Mr. Hardy said. "So far, this investigation hasn't turned up very many leads. But I've asked Sam Radley to stay in Chicago. Maybe he can turn up something."

Joe nodded. Sam Radley was an old family friend, who was also one of the best operatives in the business. He had often assisted the Hardys in solving difficult cases.

"Sam and I can handle this case from here on out," Fenton Hardy told his sons. "You've got a more important case to solve."

The boys solemnly agreed. They were now on Chet's street, and Joe pulled the van to a stop in front of the Morton home. The Hardys discussed their plan with Mr. and Mrs. Morton while Chet packed a quick bag. After a short goodbye, they piled into the van again and took off for the Hardy home. By the time they had reached their driveway, the boys noticed that the rain had stopped, and it now looked as if the sun was going to peek through the clouds.

Frank and Joe quickly packed two suitcases of their own and were soon ready to go. Their father wished them good luck as they climbed in the van and prepared for their long drive. Joe offered to drive first and slid behind the wheel, allowing Frank to stretch out in the back and take a much needed rest.

"I'll be navigator," Chet offered. He held up a stack of road maps and an auto club book for Florida. Joe smiled, and then started the van. He only hoped they would reach Florida in time to save Iola.

It was well past midnight by the time the three friends saw the Welcome to North Carolina sign along the brightly lit interstate.

"I'm starving," Chet announced, rubbing his eyes. "We won't be of any use to Iola if we've lost all our strength," he reasoned. "There's a sign for food and lodging, next exit, ten miles ahead."

"Sounds good to me," Joe agreed. "We can use some gas anyway."

"What time is it?" Frank asked. He stretched and yawned.

"Breakfast time," Chet told him.

"It's time for both of you to watch out the back window," Joe said seriously. "You remember that black-and-silver four by four that almost hit us in the airport garage? It could be a coincidence, but a

14

truck exactly like it's been following us since some-place in Virginia."

"Can you make out the plates?" Frank asked, suddenly alert. Chet crawled into the back of the van and looked out the window.

"No," Joe answered. "It's too far back for me to see."

"I can't see anything from here, either. Maybe he's going down to Florida, like us. It's probably a coincidence," Chet offered.

"I don't think so," Joe returned. "When I speed up, he speeds up. I slow down, he slows down. If he's not following us, he's doing a good imitation."

At the end of the exit ramp Joe pulled the van into the nearest gas station. Adjacent to the pumps was a large restaurant, designed to look like a southern plantation house. While Frank filled the tank, Chet and Joe stood watching the road.

"There he is," said Joe as the small truck sped past the row of service stations and headed away from the bright lights around the interchange.

"It looked to me like there were two guys," said Frank.

"I thought so, too," Joe agreed, "but they certainly didn't slow down." Joe shrugged his shoulders. "I don't know. Maybe I'm letting my imagination run away with me. I'm just tense thinking about Iola."

After Frank paid for the gas and parked the van in front of the restaurant, the boys went inside and were shown to a table. Even though it was nearly two in the morning, the waitress was cheerful. She

15

welcomed them with a southern drawl, smiling as she handed each of them a menu.

"Are you still serving dinner?" Chet asked her.

"Sure," the waitress said brightly. "We serve any meal you want, any hour of the day or night."

"Wow!" Chet replied, overwhelmed.

The teens ordered, and soon the waitress brought their food. They ate in silence, each too tired to talk. Then they paid the bill and left the restaurant.

"I've been thinking," Frank said as they walked to their van. He was lagging slightly behind Chet and Joe. "Our friends in the four by four may turn up again."

"And with friends like that, who needs enemies," Joe said, anger and impatience in his voice.

"Oh, no!" Chet moaned. He and Joe were staring at the van.

Frank didn't immediately see what they were so upset about. The van looked fine to him, although he did notice that it seemed a bit lower than usual. Then he saw why. The van was resting on its rims. All four tires had been slashed.

3 The Vanishing Trees

"They'll pay for this!" Joe vowed, staring at the shredded rubber tires.

"But we're going to have to pay first," Frank reminded him. "There's a twenty-four hour service center across the road. Let's see what kind of deal we can work out for four new radials."

"Five," Chet corrected him. "Whoever did this even got the spare." He pointed at the tire attached to the frame on the back door of the van.

"Either someone has a really warped sense of humor," Frank said, "or they're trying to scare us back to Bayport."

"It's going to take more than a few flat tires to stop us from finding Iola," Joe said. "We're going to find her no matter what."

Forty-five minutes and a couple of hundred

charged dollars later, the trio was back out on the interstate, rolling on into the morning.

"Are we there yet?" Joe asked the navigator.

Chet studied his map. "Only another three hundred miles to the Florida border," he told the Hardys.

"How far is Gull Island after we get to Florida?" Frank asked.

"I'd say we should be there by nine or ten tonight," Chet said. "The place really sounds great," he added, and began reading from his auto club book. "'Gull Island, population five hundred and thirty-seven, located only minutes off the southwestern coast of Florida between Sarasota and Naples, may be reached from any direction by boat, and by car from Seaview, across Flamingo Pass via the Island Causeway. The island features a secluded white sand beach at its southern tip.'"

"Is there a listing in there for the Royal Palms Motel?" Joe asked.

"Yes," Chet said, turning the page in the travel book. "'On Gull Island's scenic northern point. Twenty modern units with air conditioning and TV. Close to beach, shopping, and nightlife.'"

"I thought the guide said the beach is at the *south* end," Joe said. "But I guess on an island that size, everything is close by."

Finally, after nearly thirty hours on the road, the van rolled across the narrow island causeway.

"Read that part again about the nightlife," said Frank, looking at their stark surroundings.

18

"There's the nightlife," Chet said, pointing at a building. "Bud's Diner over there is open."

Frank and Joe chuckled. Bud's, Frank saw, was an ancient cinder-block and white frame building. It stood at the corner of the causeway and Gull Island's main street, Curlew Road.

"Some nightlife," Frank said.

"There's the sign we want," Joe said, pointing toward the Gull Island Marina. " 'Royal Palms Motel, four miles.' Turn right."

"They've had quite a storm down here, too," Frank observed. He steered the van around an obstacle course of downed palm trees and smashed coconuts.

"It probably looks different in the daylight," Joe commented, "but right now this island looks really run-down and deserted. There aren't many houses on these streets."

"Yeah," Chet agreed. "It's kind of creepy, as if they started to build it up, then for some reason they stopped."

"But you've got to admit that some of it still looks like postcard material," Frank said. For every palm tree blown over by the storm, he could see many more of the graceful trees standing, and up ahead was the Gulf of Mexico under a full moon.

"Finally," Frank said as they completed a sharp turn. He wheeled them past the pink neon Vacancy sign and pulled up in front of the Royal Palms Motel's office.

"It's easy to see why it's called the Royal Palms,"

19

Joe commented, straining to look up at the grove of very tall royal palm trees on the property.

"Somebody's up," Frank commented as he set the emergency brake. "Lights are still on."

Joe glanced at his watch and stretched in preparation of getting out of the van.

"Look!" Frank exclaimed. "Over there!" He threw open his door and sprinted into the night.

Joe leaped down from the passenger side and followed his brother into the dense undergrowth behind the motel office.

"Frank?" Joe waited a moment, surveying the blackness of the impenetrable foliage.

Frank didn't answer.

"Frank!" Joe called again.

Suddenly Frank emerged from the darkness and into the bright moonlight.

"There was someone behind the office, standing by that window." He gestured behind him. "When he saw us pull in, he started to run."

Joe's shouts had alerted the inhabitants of the motel. A tall man in his sixties, sporting a gray beard, came out onto the office porch. An attractive young woman followed close behind.

"Hello, there," the man hailed them. "You must be the Hardys."

"That's right," said Joe. He and Frank hurried over.

"I'm Regis Garnett," he said, shaking hands with Frank, then Joe, "and I guess you know Daphne from school."

"Hi, guys," she said. Daphne Garnett was slim

and athletic looking. Her long red hair was pulled back in a ponytail, and Joe noticed that her green eyes were filled with worry.

"And this is Iola's brother, Chet," Daphne told her uncle, introducing him.

"We're sure glad you fellows are here," said Mr. Garnett. "Chet's folks phoned and said you'd be coming. From what they said, you Hardys have had quite a bit of experience solving mysteries."

"Maybe a little," Joe admitted.

"I don't mean to alarm you," Frank said, changing the subject, "but there was someone looking in a window around the back of your office. Did you hear anything, or notice anything out of the ordinary tonight?"

"No," Regis Garnett said angrily, "and I've been hoping it would be the first night I didn't. Come on in and I'll tell you what's been going on."

Frank followed Mr. Garnett, leading the others into the brightly lit motel office. The Formica counter and the red plastic furniture were scuffed and worn, Frank noticed.

"My apartment's in back," Mr. Garnett said, holding open the drape covering the doorway immediately beside the row of mailboxes. Frank noted that most of the slots contained keys.

"This used to be a quiet little resort," Mr. Garnett explained sadly while Daphne helped him cut thick slices of a Key lime pie. "We attract the kind of tourists who want to get away from it all. Up until now we'd managed to make a fairly decent living. But that was before the so-called accidents."

21

"Yeah," said Daphne, "like the yellow racing boat that demolished Uncle Regis's dock."

"The worst part," Mr. Garnett fumed, "is that two guests were sunning themselves on the dock when it was hit. Both of them had to go to the hospital."

"What happened to the person operating the boat?" Frank inquired.

"That's a good question," Mr. Garnett said disgustedly. "Witnesses saw him push the throttle lever forward to full speed, then he jumped clear. The police discovered the boat was stolen, and nobody's seen the guy since he went into the channel. If he drowned—and I don't for a minute think he did—he'd be fish food by now."

"This happened *before* Iola disappeared?" Joe wanted to know.

"The day before," Daphne said. She opened her mouth to say something more but quickly closed it. Joe stared at her for a moment, waiting for her to continue, but she remained silent.

"Tell us what you know about Iola's disappearance," Joe prompted.

Daphne hesitated, then began her story: "I told Iola I was going to the beach at the other end of the island. I'm sort of into keeping fit, so I decided to run to the beach. It's only a few miles.

"Iola said she had some things to do, but she might join me after lunch. When she finally did decide to come out, she borrowed Uncle Regis's car. But she never got there."

"Deputy Bucknor—that's our local police force," Mr. Garnett said contemptuously, "found the car abandoned out on Pelican Lane. He did check it for fingerprints, but the only ones he found belonged to the three of us and the guy at the garage who's made a career out of working on the engine."

"There's only one police officer on this island?" Joe asked.

"That's it," Mr. Garnett answered. "Seaview—that's the county seat—assigns *five* deputies over on Castello Key. We get only one."

"Did this Bucknor find any clues?" Frank wanted to know.

"Not a thing," Mr. Garnett replied. "The car's parked out back of the office. You're welcome to look it over. Tear it apart, if you have to."

"There's been no ransom note?" Joe asked. "No unusual phone calls?"

"Nothing," said Mr. Garnett. "But then, I'm not a rich man. And what I do have, somebody's stealing. They got two of my palm trees three nights before Iola disappeared."

"Somebody stole your palm trees?" Chet asked incredulously. "Why would anyone steal trees?"

"There's a palm fungus down here in Florida," Mr. Garnett explained. "A lot of trees are dying, and some folks will pay big money for full-size replacements."

"You'd think they'd have to use heavy machinery, but we never heard a thing," Daphne put in. "The next morning I didn't even notice the trees

23

were gone until Uncle Regis saw the holes in the yard."

"I've spent my whole life here, and we never so much as locked our doors," Mr. Garnett sputtered. "Now, all of a sudden, you'd think Gull Island was a big city." He sighed and looked disgusted. "Hey, that's enough of my problems. I expect you fellows are worn out after that long drive. Let's all get a good night's sleep."

"Don't worry, Mr. Garnett, we'll look into what happened to your trees as soon as we find Iola," Frank assured him.

Joe nodded and helped Daphne gather up the pie plates.

"There's no need to be formal around here," Mr. Garnett insisted. "You fellows just call me Uncle Regis." Uncle Regis walked into the office, and the four teenagers followed. He reached into one of the mail slots, took out the key to unit 10, and handed it to Frank.

"It's down on the end," he added, waving good night. "Daphne and Iola are in unit three. It's closer to the office."

"Thanks, and good night, Uncle Regis," Chet called.

"We'll walk you to your room and make sure you're locked in," Joe told Daphne as they left the office.

"Thanks, guys. I'm so relieved now that you're here."

"Don't worry," Joe reassured her. "We'll find Iola."

24

The Hardys and Chet wished Daphne good night and waited until they heard the safety chain on her door slide into its bracket.

The boys quickly grabbed their suitcases from the van before entering their spacious room.

"I've never been so exhausted in my life," Chet said, collapsing onto one of the queen-size beds in unit 10.

"Better sleep while you can," Joe recommended, "because Frank and I plan on being up by seven to check out that old car Iola was driving."

"Me, too," Chet agreed. "Get me up even if you have to yell in my ear."

Frank was shaking his head and chuckling when the quiet of the night was interrupted by a loud shattering of glass. His eyes darted to the front window.

"What was—" Joe asked, staring for a moment at his brother.

There was a short pause, then the three boys heard a horrified, piercing scream.

4 A Million Dollars

"Your van!" Daphne shrieked from her motel doorway. "Someone's breaking into your van!"

The boys ran out of their room. Chet rushed to Daphne's side while Frank and Joe hurried to the van.

"There he goes!" shouted Joe. He raced up the road after the swiftly fleeing figure. Frank followed his brother.

"He got away," Joe gasped.

"Whoever he was broke the window on the passenger side of our van," Frank reported.

The brothers jogged back to survey the damage. Chet and Daphne were already taking inventory.

"He got the car phone," Chet informed the brothers. He held up one end of the connecting wire. "Your new fax machine's still here. Daphne scared him off before he found the locker."

"And we won't give him another opportunity," vowed Joe. He unlocked the sturdy wooden box and rescued the facsimile machine.

Frank unpacked everything else of value from the van, including a portable computer. He handed the things to Joe, who piled them in one corner of their motel room. Then the brothers cleaned away all the broken glass and covered the opening with a sheet of plastic. Saying good night to Daphne once more, Frank, Joe, and Chet returned to their room.

"Something's definitely up," Frank announced. "Iola's been kidnapped, and someone's trying to stop us from finding her."

"You're right, Frank," Joe said. "But I suggest we catch a few hours of shut-eye before we start investigating."

With that the three turned in and finally got some much-needed rest.

Early the next morning, Frank and Joe searched the rusting car Iola had been driving when she disappeared. The old heap was behind Uncle Regis's office, away from public view.

"Look at this," Joe said. His attention had been drawn to a woven nylon strap. It was caught in the glove compartment hinge.

"Does it look at all familiar?" Frank asked as he looked under the front seat.

"No, it could be a strap from anything, I suppose—a tape player, a camera."

"How about *this* camera?" Frank asked triumphantly. With one hand he held up a bright yellow sport-style camera. His other hand held out the metal ring attached to the shredded remnants of a nylon strap.

"Find anything?" Chet wanted to know as he walked up to the car.

Frank showed Chet the camera.

"That's Iola's camera!" he exclaimed.

"I figure she had to take a picture real fast," Frank said. "The camera strap got snagged in the hinge, so she jerked it out, snapped the picture, then shoved it under the seat. It was wedged in the springs."

"Chet, we need some help," Joe said to his friend. "We have to get this film developed. Drive the van over to the mainland to one of those one-hour places."

"You got it!" Chet said as he ran over to the van. "Should I get the window fixed while I'm in town?"

"Let's hold off until we have more time," Joe said. "There's more plastic in back in case it rains."

"I think we should drive out to Pelican Lane," Frank suggested as the brothers watched Chet drive off. "We ought to look over the area where the car was abandoned."

"I agree," said Joe. "It doesn't sound like Officer Bucknor made a very thorough search."

Frank and Joe borrowed Uncle Regis's car and headed for the scene of the crime.

"According to what Uncle Regis told us, this is the spot," Joe decided several minutes later as he pulled off the poorly paved road onto the sand. Frank familiarized himself with the tire treads on the old car, while Joe scoured the lot.

"We're looking for any kinds of marks in the sand," Frank said. "Maybe we can find a link to the car the kidnappers used."

"There are so few houses on this road," Joe observed, "I wouldn't think this area has been disturbed at all since Iola's kidnapping. We should be able to find something."

Frank was making a sketch of several different tire tracks when a light blue and tan police car pulled up. He watched a muscular police officer ease himself out from behind the wheel.

He sauntered over to Frank with both thumbs in his gun belt. "Name's Bucknor," the man stated, "Deputy Sheriff Bucknor."

Joe walked over to the officer from where he had been searching at the back of the lot.

"You boys lose something?" Officer Bucknor wanted to know.

"We sure hope not," Joe replied. "I'm Joe Hardy." He held out his hand as he introduced himself. Deputy Bucknor's hands stayed at his side.

"Joe Hardy?" Bucknor asked, looking slightly confused.

"That's right," Joe said, "and this is my brother, Frank."

"Frank and Joe Hardy—I believe Regis Garnett mentioned you. You're here about that missing girl."

The Hardys nodded.

29

"That girl isn't any more kidnapped than I am," the policeman snapped, "so you might as well just go back up North."

Frank controlled his annoyance and asked, "How can you be so certain Iola simply wandered away on her own?"

"You don't see anyone demanding any ransom, do you?" Officer Bucknor said.

"People aren't always kidnapped for money," Joe offered. "There could be other reasons."

"Yeah, well I don't think any of them apply here," Bucknor insisted. "But one thing I *do* know —you're standing on private property."

"We aren't harming anything," Frank pointed out.

"Doesn't matter," Bucknor insisted. "This property belongs to a local person, and I know for a fact she doesn't want strangers on her land."

Joe looked around. "It's not posted."

"A person doesn't need to have any No Trespassing signs in *my* jurisdiction," Deputy Bucknor announced.

"Perhaps if we spoke with the owner," Frank suggested.

"Never mind that," drawled Bucknor. "Leona Max has more important things to do than talk to a couple of out-of-staters who haven't got any business here, anyway. This is a nice, peaceful tourist spot."

"Friendly, too," Joe said sarcastically.

Frank started toward the car. "Come on, Joe," he

urged. "We're keeping Deputy Bucknor from his other peace-keeping duties."

Joe gave Bucknor a hard look before he followed his brother to the car. Pulling the car back out on the road, Frank noticed that Bucknor followed them as far as town.

"There goes our police escort," Frank reported.

Bucknor headed off toward the beach when Frank pulled into the lot next to Bud's Diner.

The boys jumped out of the car and stepped inside the small diner. The only customer, a well-dressed woman with bleached blond hair, was having a cup of coffee at the counter. Frank led Joe to a red leather booth directly across from the counter.

As soon as they sat down, a gray-haired waitress who appeared to be in her early fifties approached their table.

"We don't need menus, Arnetta," Joe said, noticing the name stitched on her powder blue uniform. "I'll have eggs, home fries, and toast."

"No home fries," Arnetta said. "Hash browns."

"That's fine," Frank said. "I'll have the same."

While they wolfed down their breakfast, Joe noticed a man storm into the diner through a narrow back door. The name sewn on his stained and frayed apron was Bud.

"Hey, Arnetta, you can fire up the second grill now," Bud said. "I got the lines replaced." He wiped his greasy hands on his apron. "If that deputy doesn't find out pretty soon who's going around the island destroying property, I may have to run for sheriff myself in the next election."

The blond at the counter looked up. "Give me a break, Bud," she said.

"I just might do it!" Bud exclaimed.

"Harry Bucknor's been deputy for sixteen years now," the woman said. "You've got about as much chance defeating him as you've got making this decrepit old diner turn a profit."

"The only reason Bucknor keeps his job is he's never had any actual crimes to solve, Leona, and you know it's true. Now that real things are happening, he hasn't got any idea what to do."

Leona! Frank's fork stopped in midair, and Joe turned to stare.

"You can get out from under this losing diner business any time you want," Leona said. "I've told you the development company I represent is willing to buy your little property here."

"And Bud's told you he isn't interested," Arnetta butted in, waving her spatula.

"Arnetta's right!" Bud sounded exasperated. "I have told you time after time, *I am not interested.* I appreciate your business, but you're going to have to stop pestering me about selling my restaurant."

"Bud," Leona said, "how in the world can you go on making a living selling coffee—with free refills —and a couple plates of eggs? I'm a businessperson. I know it can't be done. So why don't you just name a price?"

Based on this first impression, Frank decided he

didn't like Leona very much. Another impression he had was that Bud didn't like her, either.

"All right, Leona," Bud said slowly, "you want this place, you can have it."

"No!" Arnetta interrupted.

Bud cut her off. "Stay out of this, Arnetta!"

Frank and Joe stopped eating and focused their attention on the drama at the counter.

"That's more like it," Leona said, smiling. She opened her leather purse and took out her checkbook. "How much do you want?" she purred.

Bud surveyed his domain. "A million dollars," he said solemnly.

"A million dollars!" Frank said under his breath.

"A million dollars?" Leona Max shaped the words carefully, as though she were not sure she had heard correctly the first time.

"That's what I said," Bud repeated clearly. "I want a million dollars!"

"But of course!" said Leona Max.

Without any further hesitation, she uncapped her pen and began to write.

5 Bared Fangs

"I've got to see this," Joe Hardy said excitedly. "I've never seen a check for one million dollars."

"Who has?" Frank asked him.

"You'd better hurry, then," Bud said to the Hardys, "before I tear it into a million pieces."

Leona Max gasped when Bud took the check from her and did just that.

"Can't you take a joke?" Bud asked Leona, but before he could finish the sentence, she stomped out the front door.

"Oh, mercy, what a relief!" Arnetta exclaimed.

"I'm not selling this diner for *ten* million dollars," Bud assured her.

"Excuse me," Frank said as he and Joe walked over to the counter, "we couldn't help overhearing.

34

Does this Leona by any chance own a vacant lot here on Gull Island?"

"A vacant *lot?*" Arnetta hooted. "Leona Max owns half this island!"

"Actually, it's the real estate development company she works for that holds most of the titles," Bud corrected. "The company belongs to Vincent Vollrath. He lives down at the end of Curlew, near the beach. He's rich enough to buy about anything he wants."

"Yeah," Arnetta added in disgust, "and one of his properties is Leona Max."

"Why do you think they're trying to buy you out?" Frank asked.

"Condos," Arnetta snapped.

"That's one rumor," Bud admitted. "Gull Island's always been the poor neighbor to Castello Key. Castello's entire western shore is right on the gulf and has those great white sand beaches all around, but it's all built up now. Developers like Leona want to turn our little island into another Castello Key. The other story I'm hearing is that Vollrath wants to turn Gull Island into a private resort. You'd have to be a member just to come out here."

"A million dollars for your restaurant is a lot of money," Joe pointed out.

"I wouldn't mind giving up the restaurant, but I don't want to be run out of my home," Bud explained. "Most of the people here have been on the island for years. Gull Island's off the beaten track, and that's exactly what we like about the place."

35

"You think Vollrath's the one trying to run you out?" Frank asked.

"What would *you* think," Bud shot back, "if all of a sudden people are being burglarized and vandalized—"

"And kidnapped," Joe added.

"Yeah, I heard about that young woman," said Bud, "and I'll bet Deputy Bucknor hasn't done anything about it, either. Is that why you boys are here?"

Frank nodded. "I'm Frank Hardy, and this is my brother, Joe. We drove down here last night, with our friend Chet Morton, to find out what happened to Iola—"

The sound of tires braking hard on gravel interrupted their conversation. A door slammed, and seconds later Chet Morton, already out of breath, ran inside the diner.

"Saw Uncle Regis's car out front," Chet gasped, handing the freshly developed photographs to the brothers.

"That was quick," Frank said.

"Let's go over to the booth and take a look," Joe said. "Excuse us, Bud." The boys returned to their booth, sat down, and spread the photos across the table.

"Here's a good one of Iola and Daphne in front of Uncle Regis's old wooden cabin cruiser," Joe noted, looking through the snapshots. "Looks like your usual vacation snaps."

"Except for this one," Frank said excitedly, holding up the last picture.

36

The trio frowned as they studied the shot, turning it every which way to see if it made any sense. The photo was of the back of another car, taken from inside of Uncle Regis's car. Because Iola had apparently taken it in such a hurry, it was hard for the boys to make out all the details.

"Look," Frank said, pointing at the photo. "This is the windshield molding in Uncle Regis's car, and that's the car's hood."

Joe and Chet leaned in for a closer look at the blurred picture. "And that would be the bumper and back end of another car," Joe concluded.

"Right," Frank agreed. "And look here. There's a tiny black-and-white sticker on the lower left side of the bumper. It looks like an identification number of some kind."

"Rental cars have those!" Joe pointed out triumphantly. "It's how they keep track of their inventory."

"We've got to get this enlarged," Frank told Chet. "This could be the car that was used to kidnap Iola. If we can figure out this code number . . ."

Chet didn't need to hear anymore. He grabbed the photos and eased himself out of the booth. "I'm out of here. I'll be back with the enlargements within the hour."

"In the meantime I think Joe and I will hit the beach." Frank winked at his brother.

"What?" Chet gasped. "You two are going to catch some rays while my sister's life is in danger?"

"Not exactly," Joe explained, sliding out of the

booth. "Iola was on her way to the beach when she disappeared. Who knows what we'll find?"

Frank settled the bill with Bud and then followed Chet and Joe outside. Chet took off in the van, while the Hardys got in Uncle Regis's car. Frank started the motor and turned south on the island's main road toward the beach.

"Just like a postcard!" Joe whistled as they rounded a bend and saw the beach framed by towering coconut and royal palm trees.

"Now we know where the five hundred and thirty-seven residents are," Frank said, pointing to the crowded beach.

"They've got a perfect day, that's for sure," Joe noted.

Frank parked the car in the shade bordering the sand. Then he and Joe got out to look around.

Joe was startled by the roar of a powerful engine coming down a narrow lane behind them. Suddenly, a small black-and-silver truck was bearing down on them.

"Hit the deck!" Joe screamed.

Joe felt metal brush his leg as he jumped out of the way of the speeding truck. Tumbling onto the shoulder, he saw the driver swerve into a narrow lane that disappeared onto private property.

"That guy sure was in a hurry," Joe observed, standing up. Frank had also taken a hard fall but was already back on his feet. The Hardys brushed themselves off.

"Did you notice what that clown was driving?" Frank asked.

"You're right!" Joe exclaimed. "It was the four by four that's been tailing us, or one just like it."

"I couldn't make out the license plate number," Frank said, shaking his head. "Too much dust."

"It's a small island," Joe reminded Frank. "He'll turn up again. Let's go see what we can find."

Daphne had told the brothers that she and Iola usually sunned themselves to the right of a clump of palms near the water's edge.

"Right about here," Joe indicated, making a large X in the sand with his sneaker. He shaded his eyes and scanned the beach.

"That must be the Vollrath place," Frank guessed, looking over at a large pink stucco house set on a broad expanse of perfect green lawn.

Joe whistled. "Some shack." In addition to the three-story house, Joe saw a guest house, a five-car garage with a black sedan parked beside it, and several dog kennels. More unusual, however, was the small helicopter parked on a concrete pad.

"Vollrath must have a pretty good job," Frank said. "Strange, Daphne didn't mention anything about this place."

"We'll have to ask her if they ever met anyone from up there," Joe suggested.

The brothers walked over to a low wall that marked the edge of the public beach. Joe studied the stout chain strung between large metal posts. There was a No Trespassing sign attached to it.

"What do you think?" Joe asked teasingly. "Is a missing person investigation more important than a No Trespassing sign?"

"I've always thought the beaches belong to us all." Frank chuckled. "Besides, we only want to be neighborly."

With Joe following, Frank stepped over the chain. They made their way across Vollrath's beach.

"The worst that can happen," Frank was commenting as he hopped up onto the lawn, "is he'll tell us to get off his proper—"

Frank hesitated. He heard the enraged barking before he saw where it was coming from. He did not have to wait more than a few seconds to find out. As he began moving again in the direction of Vollrath's patio, three snarling Dobermans, fangs bared, appeared from around the side of the house.

"Frank!" Joe exclaimed.

But Frank didn't have time to react. Vicious dogs were tearing across the lawn. The dog in the lead, a huge black-and-brown beast, bore down rapidly, heading straight for Frank!

6 Portrait of Fear

"Run, Frank!" Joe yelled. He sprinted toward the beach, hoping his brother would follow his lead. He jumped up onto the stone wall and turned to see if Frank was with him.

Putting on a burst of speed, Frank tried to distance himself from the ferocious animals, but he could still feel the dogs snapping at his heels. He knew he and Joe had only one chance.

"Get ready!" Frank called as the brothers neared the wall separating Vollrath's property from the beach. "We'll have to jump for it!"

At the instant the dogs leapt in for the kill, Frank dived over the wall. Seeing his brother's move, Joe somersaulted from the wall down onto the sand at the foot of the wall. The Hardys ducked, and the dogs sailed over their heads, continuing out onto the beach for several yards.

"They'll be back!" shouted Frank.

Frank, then Joe, vaulted back up onto the Vollrath lawn. They raced toward the patio.

A brown blur in his peripheral vision told Frank the vicious dogs had turned around. He knew they would close in rapidly.

"Hurry!" Frank gasped.

Joe hurdled the shrubbery around the patio and was about to strike the nearest Doberman with an aluminum lawn chair when the sliding glass door leading into the house opened.

"Stay!" a tall, sun-tanned man commanded sharply from the shadows in the doorway. The dogs stopped instantly, then cowered at the sight of their master.

When the man stepped into the sunshine, Joe saw that he was frowning. Upon seeing the Hardys, the man grinned. But as Joe took in the rest of the man's face, he noticed his dark eyes were hard and cold.

"Nice dogs," Joe commented dryly.

"But a bit rusty." The man sighed unhappily. "They caught the last trespassers."

"We'll give them a head start next time," Joe promised him.

"Vincent Vollrath," the man announced, ignoring Joe's smart remarks, his hand extended.

"Frank and Joe Hardy," Frank responded, shaking his hand.

"Yes, I know," Vollrath said.

"Really?" Frank wondered. "How?"

"I have my sources," Vollrath said slyly. "And what brings you to Gull Island?"

"A good friend of ours is missing," Joe explained. "Iola Morton. We think she might have been kidnapped."

"That's a pretty serious charge," Vollrath said, still grinning. "But there's no reason to stand out here in this heat. Would you like a cold drink?"

Although Frank didn't particularly want a cold drink, he did want a chance to look around. "Yes, thank you," he responded.

"You'll have to excuse the mess," Vincent Vollrath said as he led the brothers through a lavishly furnished sun-room into a large kitchen. Frank noticed that the stark white counter space was piled with boxes and brown paper bags. "We're having a little party tomorrow afternoon," Vollrath said, gesturing at the clutter.

Vollrath spoke into an intercom, and moments later a tough-looking man entered the room. Frank figured he was about five foot ten. His dark face was unshaved, his hair rumpled. Frank also couldn't help but notice the muscles that rippled under his T-shirt.

"Russell Murray," Vollrath announced. "Frank and Joe Hardy."

"These are the guys I almost ran over," Murray said, as though it had been a big joke. "You boys should be more careful when you're out walking," he advised.

"That's a good-looking four by four," Frank

43

commented. "We've seen a lot of them out on the road recently."

"Never mind," Vollrath interrupted. "Get the boys some soda."

Russell Murray got four cans of soda out of the huge refrigerator.

"You sure have a great house," Joe said admiringly. "And I really like these black appliances." He walked over to Murray and took a can of pop. As he raised the can to his lips, something amid the coupons, notes, and receipts on the refrigerator door caught his eye. A shock of surprise jolted through him.

"This was taken just last week," Frank was saying as he offered Vollrath the snapshot from Iola's camera. Vollrath barely glanced at it.

"Sorry," he said, "I've never seen this young woman." Frank handed the photo to Murray.

"Nah, hasn't been anyone like that around here," he agreed, then looked at the picture.

"Iola and her girlfriend sunbathed quite a few times right out there on the beach." Joe gestured toward the water. "You're sure you didn't notice them?"

"A pretty brunette like that?" Russell Murray grinned. "I'd have remembered."

Although Joe had recovered from his earlier surprise, he thought he flinched when a phone rang somewhere upstairs in the house.

"Keith, get that!" Russell Murray screamed.

The ringing was replaced by running footsteps.

"Boss! It's for you!" a second Vollrath associate

44

shouted as he scuttled into the kitchen. He was short and very thin, with greasy black hair combed straight back. "I was putting the dogs in the kennels," he said. "It's your call from Miami."

Vollrath cut the man off. "Thank you, Keith." He turned to the Hardys. "Frank and Joe Hardy, Keith Oates."

Oates eyed the brothers nervously but said nothing.

"Listen," Joe said crisply. "We know you're busy here, so we'll just be on our way."

Frank was not quite ready to go. He was hoping that if they stayed a bit longer, they might learn something more. They had already tied the 4 x 4 to Vincent Vollrath.

Joe ignored Frank's glance. "Thank you very much for the soda," he said, "and for calling off your dogs."

"That's quite all right," Vollrath replied politely. "Keith, you and Russ show the Hardys out, will you, please?"

As the Hardys were thanking Russell Murray and Keith Oates for their hospitality, they heard the front door open and close. They could hear Vollrath's voice, and Frank recognized that of the other person, a woman who said, "Darling!"

Russell Murray reached past the brothers to unlatch the sliding glass door.

"What is it they say about its being a small world?" asked the woman in the kitchen doorway.

When Frank turned around, Leona Max was

staring at him. "You were in the diner," she said disapprovingly. "Are you following me?"

"I don't think so," Frank said, smiling. "We got here before you did."

"Maybe you're following us," Joe suggested.

"All right!" she snapped. "Nobody's following anybody."

"They're looking for some girl," Russell Murray offered impatiently, "and she isn't here, so now they're leaving."

Murray tried to slide the heavy glass door shut behind Joe, but Frank stopped him. Frank showed Leona Max the photograph of Iola. While she studied it carefully, Joe watched her expression closely from the doorway.

"Iola's been missing for three days now," Joe explained. "We thought maybe Mr. Vollrath or one of his men here might have seen something."

"She's a very pretty girl," Leona allowed. "And, yes, I've seen her, right out there on the beach. With the other girl in this picture."

"Did you ever see them with anyone else?" Frank wanted to know.

"No, no, I didn't. I wouldn't have noticed them probably, except the tourist business is really terrible this year, so there aren't very many people on the beach."

"Some say the tourist business has been hurt by the rash of accidents and vandalism that have plagued the island," Joe commented. "Like the damage to Bud's Diner."

46

"That old fool," Leona Max said sharply. "You'd have to be an idiot to turn down a million dollars."

"Or to pay that much," Frank remarked.

Leona Max stared coldly at Frank and Joe.

"Show them out," she ordered Murray.

"You were certainly in a hurry to get out of there," Frank said as soon as the brothers were out of earshot of the house.

"Did you see it?" Joe asked his brother excitedly.

"See what?" Frank wanted to know.

"On the refrigerator. You know, with all the coupons and magnets and stuff."

"I just noticed there were some things on the refrigerator door, that's all."

"One of those things," Joe said, "was my school picture!"

7 Dead in the Water

"Joe, the only way your class picture could be on Vincent Vollrath's refrigerator is if Iola put it there herself," Frank concluded.

"Vollrath and his men all denied recognizing her," Joe pointed out, "but they barely glanced at her photo."

"Iola was in that house," Frank said firmly, "and somehow she put that picture of you on the refrigerator as a clue. Was there anything else besides your picture?"

"Not that I noticed," Joe admitted.

"We've got to get back inside," Frank declared. "If Vollrath's behind Iola's disappearance, they might be holding her right there."

"Let's sneak in during the party," Joe urged. "With all the guests they won't notice us."

"Perfect," Frank agreed.

"In the meantime," Joe said, "we can drive back to the motel and see if Chet's back with that enlargement."

The Hardys made their way to the car and started for the motel.

"And let's talk to Daphne again," Frank suggested as he steered the car down the road. "I know she's upset about Iola, but she hasn't told us very much."

"You mean you think Daphne knows more than she's letting on?" Joe asked as the brothers pulled up in front of the Royal Palms, parking next to their van.

"She acts like she's hiding something," Frank remarked.

Chet ran up to the car before Frank had a chance to set the brake.

"How's *this?*" Chet asked proudly. He held up a cropped 12 x 14 inch enlargement of the blurry photograph from Iola's camera.

"It's one of those identification codes!" Frank said as he got out of the car.

"Most of the numbers under the bars are still out of focus," Chet admitted. "The darkroom guy told me this was the best he could do."

"It's good enough," Joe said as he got out of the car and glanced at the enlargement. "The last three digits appear to be three-two-six."

"What we need to do next is contact rental car agencies," Frank explained when they had entered

49

the motel office, "and trace the numbers until we get a match."

"I know, I know," Chet said. "It's back out on the road for Chet."

"It's out on the street for us all!" Uncle Regis sputtered angrily as he walked in from the back room. "Look at this letter." He threw it down on the counter.

"What's Independent Electronic Bookings?" Frank asked as he slipped the letter from the opened envelope.

"They've handled my reservations for years," Uncle Regis answered. "It's a toll-free number people can call to make reservations at independent motels."

"'We are suspending service to the Royal Palms,'" Frank read out loud.

"Why would they do that?" Joe asked.

"That's what I tried to find out," Uncle Regis fumed. "I just got off the phone, and they wouldn't tell me anything. I've never missed a payment to them, not one! The truth is they don't have a reason."

"Maybe someone's gotten to them," Joe said.

"I've about had it," Uncle Regis conceded. "My trees have been stolen, my dock has been wrecked, and someone is trying to do the same thing to my business! I've been offered pretty good money for this place, and I've half a mind to take it. If we don't move my boat to the marina, where they've got twenty-four hour security, I'll probably lose that, too."

"Your friend Bud's standing firm," Frank told him. "I don't think you should let whoever it is run you out."

"That's much easier said than done," grumbled the older man.

"Don't do anything today," Joe advised. "You're too upset."

"We'll help you," Frank assured Uncle Regis. "I know we're busy with Iola's disappearance, but it just may be that if we solve one puzzle, we'll have solved them all."

"Some battles aren't worth fighting," the resort manager argued. "I'm not making any promises."

"Let's plug in the fax and send Dad a message," Frank said. "He can run a check on Vollrath and Leona Max, and we can ask him to call the Mortons to keep them up to date."

"While we're at it, let's ask him for a rundown on Independent Electronic Bookings," Joe suggested.

"That Max person you just mentioned," Uncle Regis put in. "The same day Iola disappeared, that woman came waltzing in here and offered me half a million for this property! I told her I didn't want to sell."

"For someone who's supposed to be a successful real estate salesperson," Daphne added as she entered the motel office, "she sure was rude."

"Practically threatened me," Uncle Regis added.

"Well, we're going to have our father check her out," Frank said.

"Don't forget to ask him how he's doing on his case," Chet reminded them.

51

"The boat's all set to go," Daphne informed her uncle. "Everything's stowed away so we can move it anytime now." She watched intently as Frank made the fax machine hookups to Uncle Regis's phone jack.

Frank wrote out their note to his father on a piece of Royal Palms Motel stationery and then keyed in the number of their father's fax machine. There was a pause, a beep, and another short delay before the tiny screen indicated the letter had been sent.

"I'll get on those car rental places just as soon as I move Uncle Regis's boat," said Chet.

"Let's hope it will be safer at the marina," Uncle Regis said.

"I'll give you a hand," Frank offered. "Keep an eye on the fax, Joe. If Dad's in his office, we should have our answer soon."

Frank, Chet, and Uncle Regis stepped outside the motel office and looked out at the dock where the *Manatee* was moored. The Royal Palms Motel might look a bit neglected and run-down, but Frank had to admit that the *Manatee*, Uncle Regis's forty-year-old cabin cruiser, had been well maintained.

"Aren't very many like it left in Florida, or anywhere else, for that matter," Uncle Regis said, looking out at the sleek boat. The hull was white and gold, the decks and trim glistening mahogany.

"Is it fast?" asked Chet.

"It was in its day. Has an old straight-eight-cylinder engine, very powerful! But these new fiberglass jobs are a lot faster," Uncle Regis admitted.

52

"But they don't have the character," Frank said, admiring the *Manatee*. Uncle Regis smiled and patted Frank on the back before returning to the office.

"I'll steer!" Chet announced as he ran down the path and leapt up onto the polished deck.

"Then I guess I'll unfasten the lines," Frank said, jogging over to the boat at a more leisurely pace. "But I get to steer next time!" he shouted.

While Frank worked at the knots and coiled the lines before pitching them into the boat, Chet climbed the short ladder up to the bridge and slipped behind the wheel.

"Let's check out what this baby sounds like!" Chet called as he turned the key to start up the motor.

But instead of hearing the purr of a perfect engine, Frank heard the horrifying roar of a powerful explosion as it ripped through the deck of the *Manatee*.

The mighty force of the blast knocked Frank off the dock, sending him headfirst into the debris-ridden water near the back of the boat. Almost instantly the once proud craft began to tilt on its side.

Flames and acrid black smoke poured out of the *Manatee*'s engine compartment, choking Frank as he poked his head out of the water and tried to breathe. He couldn't see through the smoke. Where was Chet?

"No, no!" Frank heard the boat's stricken owner cry out. He turned toward the sound and saw that

Joe, Uncle Regis, and Daphne were running to the dock. Uncle Regis pulled himself together, shielded his eyes, and squinted at the water. He called to Chet and Frank. Frank tried to answer, but his cries were drowned out by the crackling of the flames.

Frank recovered from the shock of being thrown and swam frantically away from a burning deck chair bobbing nearby. Why didn't Chet answer Uncle Regis's call? Chet had been at the wheel of the boat when it exploded. Where was he now?

Surrounded on all sides by smoldering flotation cushions and other debris, Frank treaded water and craned his neck, scanning the surface. No matter which direction Frank looked, he could not see Chet in the water.

He looked back at the *Manatee*. It was sinking deeper in the channel. If Chet was still aboard, he would drown.

Unless he was burned alive first. Terror and rage swept over Frank as he watched the entire deck of the doomed pleasure craft erupt in flames.

8 Stranger in Town

"Frank!" Joe shouted as he sprinted the short distance from the motel office to the water. The channel was covered in smoke and flames from the burning cabin cruiser. "Chet!"

The younger Hardy stopped at the water's edge and quickly surveyed the burning wreckage.

"Frank!" he called again. *"Chet!"*

"Over here!" Frank answered weakly. "I'm all right," he added, "but I can't find Chet!"

Joe knew if Chet was not underwater, he must still be aboard the *Manatee*—and the *Manatee* was sinking. Joe kicked off his shoes and dived into the water. A few strokes with his strong arms and he was alongside the boat. The stern was already awash.

Frank swam over, joining him.

55

"Chet was at the wheel," Frank said.

"I think I see his foot!" Joe cried, and hoisted himself up over the side of the boat. He scrambled across the treacherous deck, then disappeared into the smoke and shadows of the pilot's compartment.

"Here he is!" Joe shouted. "Can you give me a hand?"

Frank pulled himself out of the water and flopped into the boat.

By this time Joe had gripped Chet under the arms. Their friend was dazed and had a nasty cut on his forehead. Frank made his way over to Joe, and together they lifted Chet out to safety.

Uncle Regis and Daphne arrived at the wreckage in a small aluminum fishing boat with an outboard motor. They helped Frank and Joe ease Chet into the skiff.

"He's breathing regularly," Uncle Regis said, relieved. He checked Chet's wrist for a pulse.

Frank and Joe swam back while Uncle Regis turned the dented old fishing boat around and motored back to shore. As he scrambled up onto the bank, Joe looked back in time to see the *Manatee*, in a turbulence of bubbles, sink to the bottom of Flamingo Pass.

Chet, aided by Daphne and Uncle Regis, was able to climb out of the boat and walk to the office. Daphne, a first-aid kit by her side, was already tending the cut on Chet's head when Frank and Joe returned to the motel office.

"What happened?" Chet wheezed groggily. "The last thing I remember doing . . ."

"You blew up Uncle Regis's boat," Joe quipped. "But you didn't know you were going to do it."

Chet groaned again and rubbed his head.

"There was a bomb wired to the ignition," Frank said.

"I remember now!" Chet exclaimed. "The next time we go out on a boat," he said to Frank, "you can steer."

The Hardys laughed, relieved that their friend wasn't seriously hurt. Daphne placed a bandage on Chet's cut and put the first-aid kit away.

"Are you going to report this to Deputy Bucknor?" Daphne asked her uncle, who was sitting in the chair next to Chet.

"What for?" Uncle Regis grunted. "He'll only tell me to be careful about venting gasoline fumes."

Several loud beeps from the fax machine got Joe's attention. "It's our answer from Dad," he announced, checking the machine. He removed the three-page fax from the tray.

"Dad's got his operative, Sam Radley, checking on that reservation booking company," Joe said after scanning the note, "and according to this, Leona Max is clean. Vollrath is another story. He had one conviction years ago. Since then he's been tried and acquitted three times on various charges. Dad says Vollrath's got gangland connections."

"He's currently under investigation for income tax evasion," Frank added.

"You think he's involved with all the trouble we're having?" Uncle Regis asked doubtfully.

"Why would organized crime want to blow up my boat or steal my palm trees?"

Frank shrugged his shoulders. "We don't know if Vollrath is behind the island's vandalism, or even Iola's kidnapping. At least, not yet. If only we had some concrete evidence."

Frank and Joe exchanged glances. They knew if they didn't come up with something soon, they might lose Iola's trail and never find her.

"Listen, guys," Daphne said nervously. "I really owe you an apology." She slumped in her chair.

"What do you mean?" Joe asked pointedly.

"I didn't say anything before because I felt so guilty," Daphne began, tears appearing at the corners of her eyes. "The truth is, I'm partly to blame for Iola having disappeared."

"I can't imagine you're in any way responsible," Frank told her soothingly.

"The best way to help Iola," Joe stated, "is to tell us everything you know."

"The day it happened," Daphne said, sobbing, "I went to the beach alone, and this good-looking guy with blond hair and these really pale blue eyes came over and sat down beside me."

"Murray and Oates both have brown hair," Frank noted. "What was this guy's name?"

"Brian Montrose. He told me he worked over at that pink mansion and how he'd noticed us on the beach. He said he really wanted to meet my friend. I told him Iola was planning to come out after she got some things done, but I couldn't promise anything, and besides, she already had this boyfriend at home." Daphne looked sheepishly at Joe.

"What did you think of this Brian Montrose?" Joe asked, clamping his jaw.

"He was very charming." Daphne sniffled. "He said I could use his car phone and call Iola, so finally I did. He took me over to this huge black sedan with one of those portable phones, and I made the call."

"What did she say when you talked to her?" Frank asked.

"She didn't want to come, but I reminded her we were on vacation. Finally she said okay, she'd come. The last thing she said to me was, 'You'd better never say anything to Joe Hardy about this!' "

"Tell us what happened next," Joe prodded.

"As soon as I told Brian that Iola was on her way, he said he didn't have time to sit around. He said he'd meet her some other time."

"He left?" Frank asked.

"He practically ran," Daphne said. "I didn't put any of this together with Iola disappearing until you guys got here. I remembered Iola saying when she'd been down at the marina the other day that she'd seen this hunk in a yellow racing boat." Daphne looked meekly at Joe. "She said it was probably a coincidence, but it looked like the same boat that rammed Uncle Regis's dock. She said the guy had light hair and these really unusual blue eyes."

"Then you suspect it was Brian Montrose that Iola saw at the marina," Frank concluded.

"I think so." Daphne sighed. "Of course, I know that doesn't really explain her disappearance."

"But it gives us something more to work on," Frank pointed out. "Montrose told you he works for Vollrath. That's one more clue linking Iola to Vollrath."

"It sure is," Joe agreed, "and, Daphne, I want you to know I am not upset with you about Iola checking out the guys down here."

"Joe . . ."

"I mean it," he insisted. "Case closed."

"I've got an idea," Frank announced. "Chet, if you're feeling up to it, how would you like to pay a visit to the Vollrath mansion? One of us would go, but he knows who we are."

Chet felt the bandage on his head. "I'm a willing soldier," he assured them. "No scratch is going to stop me from finding my sister."

"All you have to do," Frank explained, "is knock on Vollrath's front door, tell whoever answers you're from Gull Island Cable TV and that Brian Montrose called to request a cable hookup. Just check out the person's reaction to the name. That's all."

"That's *all?*" Chet sounded skeptical. "I mean, every time you say 'that's all,' I seem to get knocked out or tied up!"

"Look at this," Joe interrupted. He had been reading through the fax again. "Dad says they still haven't caught that gang in Chicago, but now he knows the real name of the ringleader—a man by the name of Rex Orraca."

"Anything about the phone company information you dug up for him?" Frank asked.

"Yes. He's gotten something on George Kulp. Kulp was in jail until a year ago. Dad says Kulp never had a job in his life, yet he owns that warehouse over in Miami. Dad admits Kulp could be legit, but it's more likely he's gotten in with a bad crowd."

"Sounds like you gave Dad a real lead," Frank said, complimenting his brother.

"Once we've found Iola," Joe said, "we might run over to Miami to see what we can find out for Dad."

"Good idea," Frank agreed, "but right now we've got to make sure Chet isn't late for his first cable TV customer."

The Hardys, Chet, and Daphne all piled into the van. Joe took the wheel and headed for Gull Island's small business district.

From items stored in the back of their van, Frank put together an authentic-looking cable installer disguise for Chet.

"Take the van," Frank told Chet. "Vollrath's is the only pink mansion straight down Curlew Road."

"We'll meet over at Bud's when you get back," said Joe.

"Okay. Wish me luck," Chet said as he drove off toward the beach and Vollrath's house.

"We might as well look around town while we wait," Frank suggested after the van was out of sight.

Frank led the way, wandering past the bank, then pausing at a small souvenir stand featuring jewelry made from seashells. While Daphne was checking out the merchandise, Frank surveyed the town. When he saw a nondescript green car with the bumper sticker marking it as a rental car drive down the main street, he didn't pay it much attention. The driver pulled into the gas station next to the outdoor gift shop. Frank watched as a dark-haired man got out. His pale skin revealed that he had only recently arrived in Florida. Frank overheard him tell the attendant to fill the gas tank, check the oil and tire pressure, and that he would be right back.

"Well, I don't see anything I can't live without," Daphne told the brothers as they wandered away from the stand. The trio walked on down the street, then crossed to the other side and entered the pharmacy.

Frank was slowly turning the paperback book rack when the man from the gas station walked in and stood by the prescription counter. Frank watched as the druggist greeted him warmly, but the man only grunted and passed a prescription container across the counter.

"This'll be a few minutes," Frank heard the pharmacist tell him. "I've got old Mrs. Peabody's prescription to fill."

"I can't wait all day," the man said curtly. "I have other things to do."

Frank was staring now. The man appeared not to notice, his concentration totally absorbed by a copy of *The Island Times.*

"Such a nice crowd this year," the young, pretty cashier at the counter across from the bookrack whispered sarcastically, giving Frank a knowing expression.

"I take it he's not a resident," Frank spoke confidentially. He inched closer to the counter.

"We don't have any idea who he is," the clerk reported. "Rumor is," she added in a whisper, "he's hiding out from the FBI."

"Is he staying on the island?" Frank asked as Joe and Daphne joined him at the register.

"End of Pelican Lane," the woman confided.

"Pelican Lane!" Daphne blurted. "That's where Iola's car was found!"

The man turned his head toward them quickly, then caught himself and went back to his paper.

Suddenly the drugstore screen door flew open with a bang. Everyone jumped.

"No need to get excited," Chet said, laughing. "It's only me, your friendly neighborhood cable TV installer. And let me tell you what—"

Frank and Joe both put fingers to their lips at the same time and hustled Chet outside. Daphne followed them.

"We didn't want that customer to hear what you had to say," Frank explained.

"You mean Count Dracula over at that old soda fountain?" said Chet.

"Never mind that. Did you see Vollrath?" Joe asked.

"He's a tall, mean-looking guy with graying hair, right?" Chet asked as they walked across the street.

63

"That's Vollrath," Joe confirmed.

The group stopped in front of the gas station. They took up positions between their van and the just-serviced green rental sedan.

"I don't think he suspected a thing," Chet said proudly. "I said exactly what you told me to. I told him I was there to install cable TV, including several premium channels—I threw that part in myself—ordered by one Brian Montrose on Curlew Road."

"What'd he say?" Joe asked eagerly.

"He looked downright shocked," Chet said. He paused dramatically. "Then he told me there must be some mistake, there was no such person at that address, and besides, they already had cable TV, including all of the premium channels. Then he slammed the door in my face."

"Good work," Joe told their friend. "That's the connection we've been waiting for. Montrose and Vollrath are up to something."

"It would seem so. Now if we could only find Montrose," Frank said, letting his expression go blank as the stranger from the drugstore headed in their direction from the gas station's office.

"What do you think you're doing, leaning on my car?" the man asked menacingly.

Frank and Joe tensed. Chet immediately stepped between Daphne and the man.

"We were just admiring it," Frank said, a friendly smile on his face.

"That's right," said Joe. "I understand these cars are very dependable."

"Well if you like them so much," the man said, "I would suggest you go down to the rental agency and get your own."

With that he pushed past the Hardys and got into the car. He switched on the ignition and roared away, tires squealing on the hot pavement.

"He sure seemed to be in a hurry," Chet commented.

"One thing's for certain," Frank said, smiling, "you aren't going to have to run around to all of those rental car places looking for the car in Iola's photograph."

"Why's that?" Chet wanted to know.

"Because I think we've found it."

"Where?" Daphne looked around.

"We were looking right at it," he told Daphne. "Did you happen to notice the sticker on the back fender of that green car?"

"What about it?" Joe asked.

"It was an inventory sticker for a rental car," Frank said, "and the last three digits on the identification code were three-two-six!"

9 Selling Out

"If that green rental car is the same car in Iola's photograph," Frank said, "that means our pale friend from the drugstore may know about her disappearance."

"He might even be the kidnapper." Chet shuddered.

"It's a good lead," Joe agreed. "We'll have to follow it up."

"Let's ask at Bud's if anyone knows anything more about that guy," Frank suggested.

The group entered Bud's Diner and lined themselves up along the counter.

"The man in the drugstore would be Neil Jadwin," Arnetta said in response to Frank's inquiry. "He's been coming in for a month now. Unpleasant sort. Never wants to talk."

"We heard he lives on Pelican Lane," Joe added.

"That's what they say," Bud interjected as he came out of his back office. "And they're also saying he's some kind of crook."

"I heard he's down here from Chicago," Arnetta said dramatically. "Someone told me he *killed* a man!"

"Yeah, that's one story," Bud said, chuckling. "Another one holds he's one of those spies who's had to change his whole identity because there's a foreign power out to terminate him."

"He sure looks creepy," said Daphne. "Who knows what he's mixed up in."

"There's just enough daylight left that we ought to find out for ourselves," Frank proposed.

"Let's drive out to Pelican Lane," Joe said. "There are a few things I'd like to say to Mr. Jadwin."

Frank slowed the van to well below the posted speed limit as he turned down Pelican Lane. Faded For Sale signs stood in many of the vacant lots, and the one house they passed appeared to be empty, Frank noted.

"Drive down to the end so we can look Jadwin's place over," Joe suggested. "Then we can turn around and park facing away."

"What difference does that make?" Daphne asked nervously.

Joe turned and winked at her. "We might have to make a fast getaway."

In Joe's opinion the Jadwin residence looked

more like a cottage than a house. It had a small unpainted deck jutting out from the front door and a flat roof. Floor-to-ceiling windows looked out on Flamingo Pass, giving a panoramic view of exclusive Castello Key. Much of the paint had flaked off, parched dry from seasons in the sun. The remainder of the cottage was stark, unstuccoed concrete block. Only the many graceful palm trees on the lot softened the institutional look of the building.

"Jadwin's probably home," Frank said, pointing to the rental car parked on the crushed coral drive.

"We'll know soon enough," Joe said. He jumped out of the van.

"Chet, you stay here with Daphne," Frank said. "You've had enough excitement for one day."

"Sure, Frank," answered Chet, smiling happily at Daphne.

Frank and Joe left the van and walked toward the little cottage. Neil Jadwin opened the front door before Joe had a chance to knock. Joe peered in at Jadwin, who was standing back from the door in what appeared to be a dining room.

"You again!" Jadwin shouted. "What do you want?"

"We want to talk to you," Frank responded politely. "May we come in?"

"I saw you nosing around my car. Why are you bothering me?" Jadwin stepped forward several inches, as if he meant to close the door in their faces.

"We just want to talk to you," Joe repeated.

"I don't think I have any reason to talk to you," he said rudely. "I don't even know you."

"I'm Joe Hardy, and this is my brother, Frank," Joe told him.

"A very good friend of ours disappeared down here," Frank explained.

Joe took the photograph of Iola and Daphne out of the back pocket of his jeans and showed it to Jadwin.

Jadwin gave the picture serious attention. The Hardys watched for a glimmer of recognition. Finally Jadwin looked up. "I don't know either one of these girls, and anyway, it's got nothing to do with me. Now will you please get off my property," he said.

"This is really very important," Joe persisted. He put the photo away. Then he decided to take a chance. "Did Vincent Vollrath threaten you if you didn't keep your mouth shut?"

"Get off my property!" Jadwin yelled.

Frank and Joe stood their ground.

"To tell you the truth," Frank said in a confidential tone, "we think Iola was kidnapped."

"That's right," Joe added. "By someone driving a car exactly like yours."

"I don't know what you're trying to accuse me of," Jadwin sputtered, "but I have absolutely no connections with Vincent whatever his name is. I can prove I've been here every day and every night painting my pictures. I'm an artist, you know." He stepped back into the shadows of the gloomy house and slammed the door.

69

Frank and Joe exchanged glances.

"I'll get the license number off Jadwin's car," Frank told Joe as they left Jadwin's porch. "Why don't you check out those tire tread sketches?"

Frank jotted down the information in the small notebook he carried with him while Joe examined the rental car's tires.

"One of the treads matches up with the set we found near where Iola's car was abandoned," Joe reported when the brothers rejoined Chet and Daphne in the van.

"What was Jadwin like?" Daphne asked.

"I don't know whether he's a gangster or a spy," Joe said seriously, "but I noticed he flinched when I asked him if he'd been threatened by Vincent Vollrath."

"We need to concentrate on Jadwin's car," Frank decided. "All we have is some circumstantial evidence linking a photo from Iola's camera to a rental car with the numbers three-two-six on its inventory sticker and a certain make of tires. The problem is," he continued, "there are thousands of rental cars just like Jadwin's, all with those same original equipment tires. We need to get something more definite so we can rule out coincidence."

"You mean I'm going to have to visit all those rental car places over on the mainland after all?" Chet groaned.

"I think we can do a lot of it over the phone," said Frank.

"Why don't you let me handle that," Daphne offered.

70

With that settled, the teens headed back to the motel.

"It looks like Uncle Regis has company," Frank pointed out when he pulled into the motel parking area. There was a flashy American luxury car parked outside the office door.

Daphne hopped down out of the van before it stopped moving and rushed into the motel office.

"I really don't want to sell," Uncle Regis was saying when Daphne, with the boys close on her heels, entered Uncle Regis's apartment behind the office, "but I don't see any way out of this mess, either."

Leona Max, wearing her best wheeler-dealer smile, glanced at Daphne, then at the Hardys and Chet when they gathered around the table. Quickly she turned back to business.

"This is for nine-hundred thousand dollars!" said Leona Max, sounding very impressed with herself as she waved a blue check in the air. She was sitting across the table from Uncle Regis. His head was bowed, his eyes downcast.

"You'll make ten times that much when you develop the property into condos." Uncle Regis sighed, refusing to look at both the real estate developer and her check.

"Maybe *twenty* times," Joe interrupted.

"Here, why don't you sign these forms," Leona Max urged Uncle Regis. She slid several long documents across the desk, first placing the check on top for him to pick up.

"Uncle Regis, you can't!" Daphne protested.

"What else am I going to do?" he asked dejectedly. "While you were gone, the state resort inspector was here. He says if I don't make a number of improvements in the next few weeks, he'll have to shut me down. Another inspector was here six months ago, but this fellow said the law's been changed and they're doing spot inspections. I'm tired of fighting it."

"Just sign where I've indicated, Mr. Garnett," Leona said sweetly, "and the state inspector will be someone else's problem."

She handed Uncle Regis her pen.

"Before you sign anything, Uncle Regis," Frank put in quickly, "I think you ought to read every line, maybe even let a lawyer see the documents first."

"You can make all the suggestions you want after we've transacted our business," Leona Max snapped, "and I don't mind telling you I resent the implication that this is in any way dishonest!"

"May I use the phone in your office, Uncle Regis?" Frank asked.

He waved his assent, and Frank disappeared into the next room.

"Please don't sell out, Uncle Regis," Daphne implored.

"Could I look at these?" Joe asked as he snatched up the contracts.

"Hey!" Leona Max bellowed. "You can't—"

Although Joe was hardly a legal expert, he began reading the contract.

Uncle Regis hesitated, then put down the pen. "Why can't he read it?" he asked. "If there's nothing sneaky, there's no reason for you to be so anxious."

Joe could not help but smile slightly when Leona Max abruptly snapped her briefcase shut. The woman radiated such hostility that Daphne stepped back reflexively.

"You young men have been nothing but busybodies since you got here!" Leona shouted. "That silly friend of yours is probably lying on a Fort Lauderdale beach right this minute. Why don't you all go over and join her?"

"I know you're only making a suggestion," Joe commented innocently, "but somehow it comes across as a threat."

Joe looked into the next room and saw that Frank was on the phone. His brother quickly scribbled down something in his notebook, then hung up. Frank was still reading the information when he returned to the apartment.

"I finally reached someone at the state's Bureau of Commercial Inspections. They were ready to close for the day, but I found out that the man claiming to be a state resort inspector was a phony," Frank announced. "This motel is not slated for another inspection until November."

"But he had identification," Uncle Regis explained.

"Probably phony as well," Joe pointed out.

"You're lying!" Leona Max shouted, her rage coming to the surface. "You weren't in there long enough to call anyone. I'll bet if I called that office, they never heard of you!"

"Be my guest," Frank said, moving aside so the angry woman could get to the phone.

"You meddling outsiders!" she spat at the Hardys. She grabbed the contracts away from Joe, picked up her check, and started for the door.

"You haven't seen the last of me!" Leona Max shrieked. "These are heavy hitters you're interfering with. I don't think you have any idea how serious this is. And you!"—she pointed right at Uncle Regis from the doorway where she stood—"you old fool, you'd better sell this place while you can. If you don't get out when you have the opportunity, you just may find you don't have anything left to sell!"

10 Caught in a Trap

"Do you think Leona Max had anything to do with Iola's disappearance?" Joe asked Frank as he heard the real estate woman's car roar away.

"Dad ran her through Records and Identification and didn't come up with anything," said Frank. "But we know she's connected to Vollrath, and that doesn't look too good."

"Let's keep an eye on her," Joe suggested, "but in the meantime, let's concentrate on Jadwin. We need to find out whether or not it's a coincidence that he's driving a car with part of the same bar code number that showed up on Iola's pictures."

"I'm already checking that out," Chet said as he looked through the yellow pages. "I'm marking off all the car rental agencies in the area."

Frank yawned. "Let's call it a day. We can check

out those rental companies as soon as they open tomorrow."

"And we want to make sure we're rested up for Vollrath's big party," Joe added.

"You fellows are serious about crashing Vollrath's party?" asked Daphne.

"I don't think we have any choice," Joe replied. "My picture on the refrigerator means Iola was there, and she may still be."

Frank and Joe were up early the next morning. They dressed quickly, then headed for the motel office.

Frank was pleased to see that Daphne and Chet were already on the job when he came in.

"Things are already happening," Daphne told Frank. "Uncle Regis got a call late last night from one of his card club buddies who lives over on Hibiscus Drive. Someone broke all the windows in his sun-room and smashed his air conditioner. Officer Bucknor took the report, but he said it was probably just kids."

"A person couldn't ask for a more trusting police officer than Deputy Bucknor," Joe said sarcastically.

"I've also been talking to the car rental agencies that are at the airport," added Daphne.

"Have you come up with anything?" Frank wanted to know.

"I described the car, the color, and the inventory sticker the way you said," Daphne reported. "Most of the rental car agencies carry that make and model, but only two use those particular stickers. There's a record at the agency over in Seaview of renting such a car to someone with a Gull Island address," she continued, "but they've got a company policy against giving out names."

"What about the other agency?" Frank asked.

"They rented one car that same color," Chet informed them after glancing at the legal pad Daphne had used to make notes.

"A car with a three-two-six inventory number was rented to a family from Nebraska," Daphne elaborated. "The family said they were going to visit the theme parks near Orlando."

"If we plug into Dad's computer," Frank suggested, "we can come up with a list of names of people dealing with the Seaview agency."

Joe hooked up the modem and their laptop computer. Frank keyed in the phone and code numbers that would access their father's computer in his Bayport office.

"We've got several clues to Iola's disappearance," Frank said while he waited. "First, there's the blurry photograph we're assuming she took. Then we saw Joe's class picture on Vollrath's refrigerator." Frank rubbed his forehead thoughtfully. "And the four by four that almost hit us coming out of Vollrath's driveway is probably the same one that followed us down from home."

"Don't forget Brian Montrose," Daphne reminded them.

"Right," Joe said, an edge to his voice. "We don't want to forget him."

"We've got it!" Frank suddenly shouted, momentarily looking up from the computer screen. "The Seaview agency rented the car to Neil Jadwin. The record shows his Pelican Lane address, but it says here his home address is Chicago."

"According to this," Joe added, looking over his brother's shoulder, "he's an insurance salesman. Why is an insurance salesman down in Florida painting sunsets?"

"We don't actually know he's painting sunsets," Chet pointed out.

"Maybe we ought to pay another call on Mr. Jadwin," Joe said. "I want to know why Iola took a picture of his rental car."

"Speaking of insurance agents," Daphne said, "Uncle Regis called from the mainland. He said to tell you he's getting the broken window in your van fixed. He said you can settle up with him when he gets back and go ahead and use his junker. He'll be home after he sees his insurance agent about the *Manatee.*"

"If he gets back before we do," Frank told Chet, "tell Uncle Regis thanks. Oh, and Daphne, we need you to send another fax to Dad. He might have something on Neil Jadwin."

"Since I know how to work your fax machine," Chet offered, "I'd be more helpful staying right here."

Daphne was still rolling her eyes as the Hardys left the motel office and walked to the car.

"We've *got* to turn up something today!" Joe said, frustration in his voice. "If Jadwin's involved in

Iola's disappearance," Joe added as he got into the passenger side of Uncle Regis's car, "the evidence might be right there in his house."

"What if he doesn't invite you in?" Frank asked, getting in behind the wheel.

"I'm going in, anyway," Joe said.

Frank started the car and drove across the island. Upon reaching Pelican Lane, they parked behind an abandoned house and got out of the car.

As they made their way across the vacant lots toward Jadwin's cottage, Frank looked up at the sky. The hazy morning sun had slipped behind ominous gray clouds, and the wind off the channel came whipping up the street, bending the palms and the more numerous pine trees.

"It's going to storm soon," Frank predicted.

"That might give us added cover," Joe said.

Reaching the vacant lot next to Jadwin's cottage, Frank paused. He stepped from behind a large oleander bush and surveyed the situation.

"Car's not there," he noted.

"You wait here," Joe told him, "while I move a little closer."

"Don't do anything rash," Frank warned.

"Now, I ask you," Joe said, grinning, "have you *ever* seen me do anything rash?"

Frank watched breathlessly as Joe, staying clear of the windows, came up on the side of the cottage. He flattened himself against the wall next to a shuttered oblong window.

Easing himself quietly along the wall, Joe turned and peered into the living room. Joe saw the roiling bank of threatening clouds reflected in the large picture windows. Although it was still morning, the sky reminded Joe much more of late evening.

Very cautiously Joe placed one foot on the first of the two steps to the deck. A wooden board squeaked. Fortunately the sound was immediately drowned out by the rumble of thunder.

He hesitated momentarily, then passed beneath an overhanging palm toward the cottage door. It was slightly ajar. Joe stepped across the threshold and out of Frank's sight.

He tiptoed into Jadwin's dining room area, then stopped and listened. Water was dripping in the sink on the far side of the room, but there were no human sounds.

Joe knew he had no business in this man's house. But with Iola's safety at stake, he began to search Jadwin's cottage.

Jadwin had been painting, all right, but Joe didn't think his work was any good. And there was not much of it. Joe was ready to leave when he spotted something familiar on the dining room table—a wristwatch. Joe picked up the watch, then turned it over. He was so engrossed in his find that he failed to hear the sound of a car engine outside.

Meanwhile, outside, Frank moved to a closer position, behind a grapefruit tree.

It was from his new hiding place that Frank heard the car as soon as it turned onto Pelican Lane. He started across the yard to shout a warning, but Jadwin's car was coming down the road fast. Before

Frank could do anything, Jadwin whipped the car into the driveway.

From out over the gulf thunder boomed. Large drops of rain began to fall as Frank sprinted toward the green car. As Jadwin scrambled out, the sky let loose a torrent. Although it was hard to see clearly, Frank thought Jadwin was holding something against his side. Something long and black.

Was it a rifle?

"Jadwin!" Frank shouted. Jadwin hesitated by his car. The angry expression on his face was unmistakable.

Suddenly Frank saw Jadwin's head jerk around, his attention drawn to the figure coming out of his cottage onto the deck.

"You!" Jadwin shouted at Joe, rage in his voice. "What were you doing in there?"

"Joe!" Frank yelled, gesturing toward Jadwin. "He's got a gun!" he shouted.

Frank's warning was obliterated by a resounding crack of thunder.

As Jadwin raised the dark metal rod past his face, a bolt of lightning split the coconut palm at the edge of his deck. Frank watched helplessly as one side of the smoking trunk was hurled toward the ground—straight at Joe.

11 Wish You Were Here

"Joe!" Frank cried out, watching horror-stricken as his brother crumpled beneath the tree.

Frank hit Neil Jadwin with a leg tackle that would have brought a smile to the face of his football coach in Bayport.

"Let go of me!" Jadwin shouted. "And don't bend these curtain rods!"

Frank looked down at the objects that were now on the ground beside Jadwin. "Curtain rods?" he asked in disbelief.

"These have been on order for a month," the insurance salesman complained.

"Never mind that now," Frank said. "My brother needs help." Frank led Jadwin over to Joe, who was pinned beneath the trunk. With help from Jadwin, Frank managed to hold the trunk long enough for his brother to crawl free. Joe groaned and rubbed a bruise on the back of his neck.

"I'm fine," he assured Frank. "I'm soaking wet but fine. The tree sort of glanced off my shoulder. Another couple of inches, though . . ."

A strong gust of wind brought a heavier downfall of rain. Frank looked up at the worsening storm. Thunder sounded directly overhead, and lightning flashed across the sky.

"Let's not push our luck. If we stay out here any longer, we'll be struck by lightning," Frank warned.

"If I don't have you arrested first!" a very hostile Neil Jadwin said sharply. He had picked up his curtain rods and was now rampaging toward the brothers. "The two of you are trespassing! And *you* were breaking and entering!" he said, pounding a finger into Joe's chest.

Joe grabbed Jadwin's shirt, throwing the surprised man off-balance.

"I didn't break into anything," Joe stressed as he stared at Jadwin. "The door was open."

"Okay, okay!" Jadwin conceded. "I admit it, the latch is broken."

Joe let go of Jadwin's shirt.

Jadwin rubbed his forehead nervously and grimaced. "You were still inside my house without my permission." He stepped back out of Joe's reach. "I'm going to call the police."

Frank moved between Jadwin and the open cottage door. "The car you're driving," Frank said calmly, ignoring the blast of rain in his face, "was used to kidnap a friend of ours."

"You're crazy!" Jadwin snapped.

"We've got evidence," Joe returned quickly.

"What evidence?" asked Jadwin.

"How about a photograph of your car at the scene of the crime?" Joe asked, self-assurance in his voice.

"So when you call the police," Frank insisted, "be sure to tell them you want to report a breaking and entering *and* a kidnapping."

Frank watched closely as Neil Jadwin's hostile attitude began to change. Jadwin walked over to the deck and slumped down against the railing. The roof extended over the deck and offered some protection from the rain.

"I didn't kidnap anyone," he insisted.

"We didn't say you did," Frank pointed out.

"But whoever did," Joe added, "used your rental car."

"So if it wasn't you, Jadwin, it had to be somebody you loaned your car to."

"Or somebody who stole it," he said sullenly.

"Your car was stolen?" Joe asked.

"Five days ago," he admitted. "I was down at the beach, painting."

"You paint landscapes?" Frank interrupted.

"Yeah, landscapes, whatever," Jadwin answered. "Anyway, I went back to my car and it wasn't where I'd left it. I had the keys in my pocket. So whoever took it had to have hot-wired it."

"Did the police get it back for you?" Frank asked.

"I didn't report it," Jadwin muttered.

"Then how do we know your car was really stolen?" Joe snapped.

"I guess you'll just have to take my word for it," Jadwin answered.

"Obviously you got the car back," Frank said.

"I thought it must have been some kids, you know, someone who wanted to joyride or something. Because when I walked into town, there it was, parked right in front of the police station. In a no-parking zone! Bucknor had even given it a ticket."

"Do you have the ticket?" Frank asked.

"I dropped it in the mail slot at Bucknor's office along with the fine," Jadwin said. "I was really fed up. My car was stolen, I had to walk back to town, then on top of it all, I get a twenty-dollar parking ticket! There isn't any justice," he said disgustedly.

"There is sooner or later," Joe commented.

"Look," Jadwin said, "I don't want any trouble. You've got to believe me, I didn't kidnap anyone and I don't know anyone who did. Whether you believe me or not, my car was stolen, and I got it back just like I said I did."

"We can each tell our stories to Deputy Bucknor," Frank said very seriously, "and he can decide who's telling the truth."

"Hey, look," Jadwin said, "I was a little hasty about this police business. The more I think about it, the more I don't see any reason to bother Deputy Bucknor."

"That's true," Joe agreed. "He's such a busy man."

Again, lightning and thunder crackled across the humid tropical sky. Joe gestured to Jadwin to go ahead inside, and without another word Jadwin bolted for his cottage.

"That wasn't rain on Jadwin's brow," Joe pointed out to Frank as the brothers, battling the storm, walked to Uncle Regis's car. "That was sweat."

"I don't know whether he had anything to do with Iola's kidnapping or not," Frank said, "but he acts like a man who has something to hide."

"He does," Joe said. "I found this lying on a work table." He handed a gold-tone watch to Frank. "Look familiar?"

An expression of shock and concern spread across Frank's face.

"I was with you when you bought this for Iola," Frank gasped. "You had it engraved—"

Quickly Frank turned the watch over and looked at the tiny letters on the back.

" 'To Iola from Joe,' " he read aloud.

"What do you think this means?" Joe wondered. "Did Jadwin take the watch from Iola when she was being kidnapped?"

"You know, we've been assuming Iola put your picture on Vollrath's refrigerator," returned Frank. "Maybe she planted this watch at Jadwin's."

"That could be," Joe allowed, "which means Iola was in both places. Jadwin knows more than he's telling us, but I just have a feeling he's not in on Iola's disappearance."

"Is that why you didn't confront him about the watch?" Frank asked.

"Yeah," Joe said, "that and I didn't want to hear it when he started hollering 'Thief!' Maybe Iola planted it, and he didn't know it was there. His place is really a mess. I think what we need to find out is if there's any way we can connect Neil Jadwin to Vincent Vollrath."

The brothers quickly got in the car, grateful to be out of the rain. Joe slipped behind the wheel and turned the windshield wipers on full speed. The squall continued to whip rain, sand, and leaves about the car. When he stopped at the corner of Pelican and Curlew, Frank suggested they pick up some take-out food from Bud's.

"It's the least we can do," Frank pointed out, "after Uncle Regis took our van into town to be fixed."

The rain was still falling as the Hardys walked into the diner. They placed their order with Bud and waited. Joe felt a gust of wind when someone came through the door. He looked over to see Deputy Bucknor strut inside.

"I've been looking for you," the officer said. Then, noticing the Hardys' bedraggled appearance, he broke out laughing. "You boys been playing in the mud?"

Frank and Joe looked themselves over. Their clothes were soaked through and splattered with mud. "Just doing a little sightseeing," Joe said.

Bucknor sniffed and dug his hands into his pockets. "Well, I've been doing some sightseeing, too, at the Royal Palms. Seems they've had another boating accident."

"Accident?" Joe repeated with disbelief. "That wasn't any accident! Somebody planted a bomb that was wired to go off when the ignition was turned on."

"Don't you think you're being a bit dramatic?" Deputy Bucknor asked. The hefty officer sat down on a stool near Joe.

"I suppose you think Uncle Regis's boat blew up because of gasoline fumes," said Frank.

"That'd be my guess," drawled the police officer. "It was an old boat. A lot of things could have been wrong."

"Yes, we've certainly had a few accidents here on the island lately," Bud said sarcastically as he began bagging the Hardys' order. "One more and I'd say we could get into that famous book of world records."

"You don't have any evidence that these aren't accidents," Deputy Bucknor said smugly.

"I suppose it was totally accidental that one of my propane tanks was punctured the other night and all the connecting tubes were pulled out and twisted," Bud retorted.

"Probably just a raccoon," Joe suggested dryly.

"Or an alligator," Bucknor added. "You know they cause problems down here all the time."

"Then I suppose you think that Iola's kidnapping was an accident, too," Frank said coldly.

"I'm glad you reminded me," the deputy said, swinging around on his stool. "When I was over at the Royal Palms, talking to Mr. Garnett, the young fellow that came down here with you—you know, the heavyset one? Well, he came running up all excited."

"You mean Chet?" Joe interrupted.

"Whoever," Bucknor replied. "He said he'd just gotten word from her in the mail."

"Iola?" Joe said excitedly.

"That's right," Bucknor said triumphantly. "All this talk about kidnapping is just so much nonsense. According to your friend, this Iola who's supposed to be missing is having the time of her life."

"How do you know *that*?" Joe challenged.

"There's certainly no mystery to it," Deputy Bucknor said, chuckling. "She sent a postcard!"

12 Party Time

"If this is your idea of a joke, Officer Bucknor," Joe said gravely, "it's not very funny."

"I'm telling you," Deputy Bucknor repeated, "your friend sent a postcard to her brother. If you don't believe me, then go back to the motel and see for yourself."

Frank and Joe paid for their order and ran out of the diner, straight to the car. Joe slipped behind the wheel and, putting the car into gear faster than Frank could buckle his seat belt, quickly drove away.

After pulling the car into the Royal Palms lot, Joe quickly parked, then jumped out. Frank could barely keep up as his younger brother raced into the office.

Chet and Daphne were looking over the postcard

90

when the Hardys came into the room. Joe practically ripped the card out of Chet's hands in his excitement to read it.

"This is Iola's handwriting all right," Joe conceded as he studied the postcard. It was addressed to Chet.

"It was mailed two days ago," Chet noted. "From Miami."

"I can't believe Iola would go running off to Miami without telling us her plans," Daphne murmured.

"She didn't," Joe said firmly. "She sent this card to Chet as a clue, knowing that he'd come here to look for her. Listen to what she wrote: 'This place is even better than last year. Wish you were here! Love, Iola.' That's why this card is a signal," Joe continued gravely. "Iola was not in Miami last year."

"That's right," Chet confirmed. "Our family went to Long Island for spring break last year."

"What do you think?" Joe asked, handing the card to Frank.

"The caption says, 'Miami's waterfront never sleeps.'" Frank narrowed his eyes, then suggested, "This picture might not have any significance at all. Maybe she sent the first card she found, maybe the *only* one available. It could just as easily have had sunsets or porpoises on it."

"I don't know," Joe said thoughtfully. "Iola *has* been leaving us a whole trail of clues. The photograph of the car, the picture in Vollrath's kitchen, the watch at Jadwin's, and now this."

"Speaking of Jadwin," Frank said, looking at Chet. "Did you get through to Dad?"

"Yes," he answered. "But he couldn't find anything on him."

"It looks to me," Frank concluded, "that Iola is not at Vollrath's house, or Jadwin's cottage. She's in Miami."

"Then let's hit the road!" Joe exclaimed.

"I'm ready!" Chet announced.

Frank remained in his seat.

"Exactly where in Miami are we going to look for her?" he asked Joe and Chet. "Miami's a big city."

"The waterfront!" Chet blurted.

"You may be right," Frank conceded, "but we don't have any real idea where to start."

"We can't just *sit* here," Joe objected.

"Of course we can't," Frank agreed, "and we're not going to. We're going to attend Vollrath's party and search his house just as we had planned. There might be other clues."

"You're right," Joe agreed. "For all we know, Iola might even be somewhere in that house. Once we've made our search, we can leave for Miami."

"What about me?" asked Chet.

"We're going to need your help when we go to the party," Frank told him. "How do you feel about taking a boat cruise past Vollrath's place later tonight?" Chet nodded eagerly.

"What about me?" Daphne asked.

"We can't leave Uncle Regis here alone," Frank decided, "not with what's been happening. If you see or hear anything suspicious while we're away, call the state police."

The storm from earlier in the day had subsided, but as Frank parked the van, with its glistening new car door window, behind a string of other vehicles at the side of Curlew Road close by Vollrath's fence, he noticed the sky was once again thickening with clouds. As Frank and Joe got out of the van, they could hear sounds of music and laughter drift across the lawn.

Because of the dense fog, Vollrath had turned on the floodlights. Even so, Frank noted with relief, the edges of his property were shrouded in mist. The mist and the trees would provide him and Joe with plenty of cover.

Frank had suggested they dress up for the party. He chose a conservative sport coat and slacks, while Joe was wearing one of those Hawaiian shirts with a bright tropical print.

"Let's hope we haven't forgotten how to be charming and bluff our way in." Joe chuckled.

Frank led the way, and they walked up the driveway.

He eyed several men who were standing at the front door, but they looked more like guests than the two tough guys who were Vollrath employees.

"Must be two hundred people here," Frank estimated as they strode into the front hall.

"Keep an eye out for Russell Murray and Keith Oates," Joe suggested.

"I don't see them," Frank said as he scanned the hall and living room.

"And we don't particularly want to run into Leona Max, either," Joe reminded Frank.

The brothers casually made their way to the kitchen. While Joe watched for other guests, Frank walked over to the refrigerator.

"It's gone," Frank said.

Joe glanced over at the refrigerator. "It doesn't look like anything else was disturbed."

"Let's split up," Frank suggested, "and see if we can find any evidence proving that Iola is here. You take this floor, and I'll go upstairs. Remember when the phone rang upstairs yesterday? I want to see if Vollrath has his office on the second floor."

"Be careful," Joe said as the brothers parted.

Frank walked casually toward the stairs. "Hey," someone called to him from the foyer, "Vincent will be back down in just a minute."

"I've got a message for him," Frank responded, thinking quickly. He hurried on up to the landing, then sprinted to the second floor.

The hall was empty. Frank turned right and walked down to the end. He passed three bedrooms and a bathroom. They were all empty.

Meanwhile, down on the first floor, Joe had worked his way through the living room, until he finally reached the far hallway. It led to a huge bathroom, a couple of bedrooms, and a den.

Starting in one of the bedrooms, Joe checked the walk-in closets, and the private bath. The room did not appear to have been used for some time.

The second bedroom was much like the first, except in the closet Joe found a small wooden crate bearing Oriental characters. The lid had been removed. The box contained an assortment of diodes, transistors, and what looked like computer chips.

Something on the library table in the last room Joe searched caught his eye—red sunglasses. As he walked over to take a closer look at them, he was interrupted by a voice behind him.

"I don't recall seeing your name on our guest list," Russell Murray said icily.

"That's okay," Joe said. He quickly pocketed the sunglasses, then turned around very slowly. "I really must be going anyway."

"Mr. Vollrath will give me a bonus for catching you snooping around," the hood sneered.

"Better not spend it until it's in your pocket!" Joe exclaimed as he leapt onto the library table, then right at Murray, knocking him to the floor.

Joe scrambled to his feet and ran out into the hallway. "See you later," he told the thug.

Upstairs, Frank made his way carefully from one bedroom to the next, looking for any sign that Iola might be in the house.

He crossed the hall to the left and headed toward the two remaining rooms. From one of them, the room at the end of the hall, Frank heard a voice. "Not yet," a man said gruffly. "I'm flying over later tonight, and I'll take care of it then. Do you understand me?" The voice was cold and commanding.

It was Vincent Vollrath's voice.

Frank crept closer to the open door and pressed himself against the wall.

"Your job," Vollrath continued, speaking in a sharp, clipped manner, "is to do exactly what Orraca wants you to do. Nothing more, nothing less."

Orraca! Frank couldn't believe his ears. That was the name of the man his father was tracking! Frank edged closer to the door.

"What'd I tell you?" Vollrath stormed. "I told you I'd take care of it when I got there. It has to look like an accident. That's why I told you to hire those exterminators. Did you do what I told you?" Frank was so intent on listening that he could barely breathe.

"Of course there are people down here looking!" Vollrath shouted. "What did you think—someone could just disappear and everyone would say, 'Oh, what a shame, so-and-so just disappeared'? It doesn't work like that, Weldon! No wonder Orraca sent you to work for me. He probably couldn't stand your stupidity!"

There was a pause, then Vollrath laughed heartily.

"You and who else?" Vollrath demanded. "Instead of threatening me," he continued, "you just make sure you have everything set up for the boss. And tell George he'd better do his part. You guys mess this up any more, and Orraca's going to give you early retirement—and you know what kind of retirement plan *he's* got!" Vollrath slammed down the phone.

The sounds of shouting from downstairs distracted Frank. Because he knew it might get Vollrath's attention as well, Frank began easing back toward a doorway where he could hide. But he was too late. Vincent Vollrath spotted Frank the moment he looked out his office door.

"Hey!" Vollrath shouted. "Oates! Murray!" Vollrath lunged at Frank, grabbing his lapel.

Frank pulled away, almost losing his jacket in the process. As he broke for the stairs, he heard Vollrath, still calling for his men. This gave him a head start, he hoped.

The party had been loud to begin with, but now, Frank could hear, it was in an uproar.

"He's getting away!" someone shouted.

At first Frank thought the person was talking about him. A quick look around, however, suggested it was someone else. That someone was fleeing across the back lawn, running in the direction of the beach.

Joe!

Right behind him was Russell Murray. Clearly Joe was in trouble.

But so was Frank.

"Stop that guy!" Vincent Vollrath shouted as he reached the foot of the steps.

Quickly the older Hardy scanned the mass of partygoers, most of whom were looking back at him to see what all the excitement was about. Frank had the impression they were amused.

But when the raging host sent a couple sprawling into a glass-fronted knickknack case, which shattered, screams replaced laughter.

Then a gunshot sent people scrambling.

Instinctively Frank ducked, but the shot was not aimed at him. It sounded to Frank as if it had come from outside.

Frank panicked. Russell Murray was shooting at Joe! He had to help his brother.

Out on the beach, Joe had never run faster in his life, and it was not easy to run in sand. His legs were burning as he gasped for air. Fortunately he could tell Russell Murray wasn't having an easy time running on the sand, either. Joe hoped it would affect his aim as well.

"That was just a warning!" Murray hollered above the sound of the surf.

Joe's only hope was the Gulf of Mexico and Chet Morton. If he could make it to the water, he would be less of a target for Murray's gun.

The only problem with that plan was the distance. The tide was out, and Chet was not where they had planned for him to be. Murray was closing in, and at least three hundred yards stretched between him and the water's edge.

Frank burst through the open patio doors and out onto Vollrath's patio. He jumped over a chair and dashed onto the lawn. Not very far ahead, yet too far for him to reach quickly, Frank saw Russell Murray stop. In the light of Vollrath's powerful mercury vapor floodlights, Murray gripped his pistol in both hands and assumed a firing stance. He aimed directly at Joe Hardy's back.

"This'll stop him!" yelled Russell Murray.

13 Alligator Alley

"Murray!" Frank shouted. "Don't shoot!"

Thunder crashed across the sky. Lightning momentarily exposed the drama for the crowd that had gathered on Vollrath's patio.

Frank could tell that Russell Murray had heard the command. He saw the gunman hesitate. That brief moment gave Joe Hardy the slack he needed.

Joe plunged into the Gulf of Mexico and swam furiously.

Frank had only a glimpse of Joe as he disappeared into the surf before Vollrath raced up to him. Keith Oates was close behind.

"Gotta run!" Frank told him. He faked to his left, his right, then dashed up the beach.

Oates was fast, but Frank had no intention of getting caught. He headed straight for the water.

But Oates was persistent. The hoodlum leaped in front of Frank, cutting his legs out from under him. Frank tumbled onto the beach. He tried to scramble away, but Oates had hold of one foot.

"Give it up, jerk!" Oates warned Frank as he twisted Frank's ankle.

"Hold him!" Vollrath called out. He was running over to the struggling pair.

"Sorry I can't stay," Frank told Keith. He kicked out with his free leg, landing a crashing blow to Oates's chin. The man yowled in pain.

That was all Frank needed. Immediately he was on his feet, putting as much beach between himself and Keith Oates as he could. He veered into the water but stayed in the packed, wet sand, where he could run faster.

One question kept racing through his mind—where in the world was Chet?

"You idiots!" Frank heard Vollrath rage. "They're getting away!"

The voices faded, but he could hear Keith's labored breathing. Frank accelerated, continuing on around to the side of Gull Island that, in good weather, looked across to Castello Key.

That night the weather was terrible. Through the mist, Frank thought he spotted a small boat struggling against the choppy water. It was silhouetted against a distant flash of lightning. Could that be Chet? he wondered. Frank squinted into the fog, readying himself for the next revealing bolt of lightning. When it came, he saw the boat again. He could barely make out someone hunched over the outboard and two others riding in front.

Although he was being chased, Frank cut his running down to a jog. The boat cut back its speed as well.

"Over here!" came a voice from the boat.

Frank stopped abruptly and looked across the channel. The water was rough, churned up by the brisk winds.

"Frank!" It was Chet's voice.

Frank waded out as far as he could and remained standing while the boat edged toward him.

Joe leaned out of Uncle Regis's fishing skiff and helped Frank scramble aboard.

"You look like a drowned rat," Joe noted.

"You look a little waterlogged yourself."

"How was the party?" Daphne asked from her place at the outboard motorboat's tiller.

"Daphne insisted on coming," Chet explained. "One of Uncle Regis's friends agreed to stay at the motel until we got back."

"This way, I could help with the boat," she said as thunder exploded overhead.

"Am I glad to see you!" Frank exclaimed. "Keith Oates is after me."

"We saw him," Joe assured his brother. "He's quick, but let's see if this boat is quicker."

"It's not," said Chet. "That's why I'm late. In this surf it was all I could do to get here."

Chet twisted the throttle control. The boat's stern dipped as the boat struggled forward, pushing slowly through the choppy water out into the channel.

"Head for one of those undeveloped side streets," Joe said above the roar from both the wind and the engine. "We've got to sneak back to the van and leave for Miami."

"I take it you didn't find Iola in Vollrath's house," Frank said.

"I found these." Joe held out a pair of sunglasses, the kind with bright red frames and mirrored lenses. "These are Iola's!" he said triumphantly. "She bought them at the mall the afternoon before she left."

Frank was impressed. "You've got to hand it to her," he said. "She's really left a trail."

Joe told them about searching the first floor rooms. "Russell Murray walked in on me," Joe concluded. "He recognized me, so I had to run for it."

"I saw that part," Frank commented.

"Yeah." Joe smiled and clapped his brother on the shoulder. "Thanks for saving my life."

"It seemed like the right thing to do at the time," Frank quipped. He told Joe and Daphne about the phone conversation he overheard. "Not only does this lead me to believe they've got Iola and they're holding her somewhere in Miami," Frank concluded, "but I think she's in grave danger. And get this, I heard him mention Orraca."

"That's the leader of the gang you were helping Dad track down in Chicago!" Joe exclaimed.

103

"Wow!" Daphne cried. "You guys are really getting somewhere!"

"I guess it wasn't such a bad party after all," Joe said.

"Except we still don't know exactly where to look for Iola," Frank pointed out.

"That's right." Joe sighed. "And what do you think Vollrath meant by an exterminator?"

"I don't know," Frank admitted. "That's all the more reason we've got to leave tonight."

"What about me?" Daphne asked. "I want to help, too."

"You can," said Frank. "Why don't you and Chet stake out Vollrath's place. Vollrath knows I overheard him talking on the phone. He and those goons might just decide to pull out. Use our camera with the telephoto lens. Photograph whoever comes and goes. Maybe you'll catch something we can use, especially when it's time to put together the evidence."

"You got it!" Chet said enthusiastically.

"We'll meet you back at Uncle Regis's," Joe said, "and thanks for the boat ride."

Frank and Joe hopped onto the sandy bank.

While making their way back to Curlew Road, it occurred to Joe that Vollrath might try to locate their van and use it to set a trap.

"We'd better check out the area first," he told Frank.

The Hardys approached silently, pausing every few moments to watch and listen.

"All I hear is the party," Joe declared after

watching the van for several minutes from the shadows provided by deep undergrowth.

"Listen!" Frank whispered. The sounds of laughter and music were drowned suddenly by the throb of a powerful aircraft engine.

"At least one of the guests is leaving," Joe commented, scanning the yard.

"I think it's the host," said Frank. "That's Vollrath's helicopter."

Joe watched as the helicopter rose straight up to a height of two hundred feet. Then, with its engine roaring, it turned east and disappeared into the heavy, moist air.

"When I overheard him talking on the phone," Frank remembered, "he told someone named Weldon he'd take care of something when he got there. I'd say he's on his way."

"So are we," Joe said, slipping behind the wheel. "And," he added, "that helicopter explains why we didn't find Iola in Vollrath's house. They probably airlifted her to Miami."

Joe turned the van around and drove them quickly back to the motel.

Frank and Joe went back to their room to change clothes before joining Chet and Daphne in the office. The brothers briefly outlined their plan before starting out for Miami. Chet had wanted to join them, but Frank reminded him that he and Daphne had another job to do—keep an eye on Vollrath's mansion.

With Joe driving, the Hardy van departed the Royal Palms and headed toward the causeway, taking the road leading to Florida's famous Alligator Alley.

"Let's hope the alligators are sound asleep," Joe muttered to himself.

He put the van on cruise. Alligator Alley was very narrow, however, so Joe had to stay alert to make sure the wheels stayed on the pavement. He noted there was little in the way of a shoulder, and on both sides of him the forbidding cypress swamp stretched away into the deepening gloom.

"Should take two or three hours," Frank said after examining Chet's map. "Be sure to wake me when it's my turn to drive." Frank crawled into the back of the van.

"You can count on it," Joe assured him.

Half an hour later Joe noticed headlights in the rearview mirror. A car had come speeding up behind them, then, instead of passing, it had been staying a steady couple hundred yards behind.

Suddenly the car in back picked up speed and hit the van.

"What was that?" Frank asked, appearing between the front seats.

"We're being followed," Joe told him.

"They're following kind of close, aren't they?" Frank quipped.

He scrambled around and looked out the windows in the van's back doors.

"It's one of those luxury sedans," Frank reported. "Exactly like the one parked at Vollrath's."

"And like the one from which Brian Montrose

had Daphne make her car phone call to Iola," Joe added. "Can you see who's driving?"

"No, it's too dark out here. And the car's got that heavily tinted glass."

"Brace yourself!" Frank ordered.

Once more the sedan slammed into the back of the van, but Joe was ready. He had been accelerating so the collision was not as sharp as it might have been.

"He's trying to pass!" Joe exclaimed.

Joe floored the gas pedal. The van inched ahead, but the sedan, with its multivalve engine, began to pull alongside.

"Let him get right beside us," Frank urged, "but don't let him pass. I've got an idea."

Frank watched the sedan swerve into the back quarter of the van, jolting them toward the almost nonexistent shoulder.

"I don't suppose you want me to let them push us into the swamp!" Joe shouted back at his brother.

"Hey," Frank said, "that swamp is a wildlife refuge. Alligators are an endangered species."

"Yeah, right," Joe said, most of his concentration on his driving. "If we go in there with them, *we're* going to be the endangered species!"

The driver of the sedan gunned it again. The ominous dark car gained steadily on the Hardys, then swerved, slamming into their left front fender.

The steering wheel was momentarily twisted from Joe's hands. The van rocked, then shook violently as the right wheels dropped off the pavement onto the soft sand shoulder.

"Hang on!" Joe cried as he fought for control of the wheel.

Frank grabbed hold of the back of the passenger seat to steady himself, but he could feel the van sliding along the edge of the embankment.

He knew this meant they'd lost traction, and as he was thrown against the metal side, he called out, "Crank it back, Joe! We're rolling into the swamp!"

14 The Jaws of Death

Joe had to act quickly. Another few inches and they would be over the edge, into the swamp.

Shifting the transmission into low gear, Joe jammed the gas pedal to the floor. With great concentration and skill, the younger Hardy wrestled the van back onto the pavement.

"Let the sedan come up so its windshield's right beside our sliding door," Frank instructed. He had pried the lid off a can of automotive paint. "Whether this works or not," he added, "we'll have to buy another quart of lacquer."

Once again the sedan roared up beside the van. When Frank judged it was in the right position, he wrenched the handle that controlled the side door and slid it back.

"Try to hold it steady!" Frank called to his brother.

Using the shovel pass wrist action he had learned playing football, Frank flung the glistening paint into the air. Frank held his breath while the paint seemed to hang in space. But only for a moment. The sedan's windshield drove straight into it. The wind spread the lustrous paint over the glass and roof.

"All right!" Frank exclaimed.

"Great work!" Joe cheered when he saw their pursuer's car go blind, then swerve off the road.

Frank saw the sedan finally screech to a halt at the side of the road. The trunk, he noted with satisfaction, was hanging well out over the swamp.

Joe brought the van to a stop. "I think we'd better help them," he said, bringing the van around. "It looks like a car just slipped into the swamp. You get the rope and I'll bring the cuffs."

When Joe braked to a stop, Keith Oates was calling for help. He was submerged up to his neck in the brackish water. He had jumped into the swamp, in an attempt to escape, but the water was too deep for him to wade to land.

"Save me!" Oates bellowed. "I can't swim!"

"Hey, man, I can't, either," Russell Murray, the driver of the sedan, hollered back. He had also gotten out of the car and was now stuck in some reeds, Joe noted with some pleasure.

"I can," Joe commented as he walked right up to Russell and locked a pair of handcuffs on the man before he knew what hit him.

"Help!" Keith kept shouting until he realized Frank was going to save him.

Frank threw Keith one end of the rope. "Tie this around your waist," Frank called.

"Hurry!" Keith cried, working quickly with the rope. "There's *wildlife* things in here!"

Frank hauled the hoodlum in, then deftly looped the rope, pinning Keith's arms.

"Hey!" Keith protested when Joe snapped closed the other cuff around his wrist, locking Russell and Keith together.

"I don't suppose either of you could tell us how to get to the police station in downtown Miami?" Joe asked the two thugs.

"We're not saying anything!" Russell muttered.

"Which one of you clowns stole our car phone?" Joe asked, wanting to see their reaction.

"I didn't steal any car phone," Keith told him sullenly.

"The man sneaking around the Royal Palms the other night was built like you," Frank said.

"Don't you go pinning Murray's crimes on me," Keith blurted.

"Shut up, you idiot!" Russell Murray snarled.

"In any case," Frank said, smiling, "I'm sure you won't mind if we borrow the phone in your sedan. You do have one, don't you?"

Keith started to answer, but Murray jerked on the chain.

"Of course you do," Joe continued. "That's the same car phone that Brian Montrose let Daphne use the day Iola was kidnapped."

Frank ordered the two criminals to sit on the car hood so it would not slide into the swamp while Joe removed the car phone. He called 911.

The police dispatcher gave them directions to the Miami Police Department.

The Hardys ushered the thugs into the back of the van, leaving the car at the mercy of the swamp. Frank drove the remainder of Alligator Alley while Joe guarded the prisoners.

Frank spotted the police officer waiting in front of the building by the curb.

"I'm Frank Hardy, Detective Ackers." Frank read the name off the burly man's badge. "My brother, Joe, and I have a present for you," he added.

Joe led the manacled Oates and Murray around from the back of the van.

"You can book these men for aggravated assault," Joe commented while shaking hands with Detective Ackers, "but I suspect we'll soon be able to add a few more charges."

Frank showed the detective Iola's picture and explained about her disappearance. "We have reason to think she was brought to Miami."

"That's right," said Joe. "We need a local address connected to Vincent Vollrath."

"Or Rex Orraca," Frank added. "Even Neil Jadwin, for that matter."

"So you're looking for Rex Orraca," the detective commented. "That's interesting, because we just got a bulletin from the Chicago police. They believe Orraca's setting up an operation down here."

112

"We have information suggesting that Orraca's going to be here sometime very soon," Frank told the police officer, "and Vincent Vollrath's tied in with him somehow."

"We thought there might be a chance that Vollrath owns some property here in Miami," Joe said.

"It's as easy as checking the computer," Detective Ackers said. He turned the prisoners over to a couple of uniformed officers, then led the brothers to his cubicle.

Ackers keyed in several commands. "There's nothing here on Orraca or this fellow Jadwin," Ackers reported, "but you've hit the jackpot on Vollrath. He's got a house down on Biscayne Bay."

Ackers wrote the address on a piece of paper, along with his phone number, and told the brothers if anything came up, they were to call him.

Joe took the wheel. The drive out to Biscayne featured more spectacular tropical scenery, but he was far too preoccupied with thoughts of Iola and "exterminators" to enjoy the view.

Because of the trees, shrubs, and the high wall surrounding Vollrath's property, Joe did not see the house at first. It was located at the end of a cul-de-sac. An iron gate closed off the driveway.

"Turn around and park out by the intersection," Frank suggested.

"You've got a plan?" Joe asked.

"Once we've sneaked inside, I'll see if I can put something together," Frank admitted with a grin.

Joe parked their van, and the boys jumped out.

113

"Remember," Frank said, "when we're looking around, we should act like we belong here."

"Right," Joe agreed, "and when we start climbing over that wall, let's try to look like it's the most natural thing in the world."

Except for a parked car half a block away, the street appeared deserted to Joe. The brothers walked casually past Vollrath's gate.

Joe glanced across the lawn at the sweeping circular drive that ended under an elegant portico. A helicopter, which he guessed was Vollrath's, was parked in an open area at the north end of the property. The grounds appeared to be deserted.

"Looks clear," Joe said in a low voice.

After one last check up and down the street, Joe led the way. He hurried to a part of the wall overgrown with vines and shaded by a large jacaranda tree. Frank made a foothold with his hands and was ready to give Joe a boost up when he heard a steely voice that caused them to freeze.

"Welcome to Miami," the man said. He was holding a gun. "We've been expecting you."

"Really?" Joe asked as he put his foot back on the ground. His captor was tall, deeply tanned, and, Joe noticed grimly, had blond hair and pale blue eyes. "I don't believe we know you."

"But we know *you*," the man continued. "You're the Hardy brothers. Or *were*," the man added meaningfully.

"I think you've made a mistake." Frank stared hard at the gunman.

"On the contrary," the man said, "I think *you're* the ones who made the mistake."

The man removed what appeared to Joe to be a small remote control device from his hip pocket. At the push of a button the iron gates began to swing open.

"You wanted in—now's your big chance," the man prompted, gesturing with his pistol.

The gunman jabbed the pistol into Joe's back, pushing the younger Hardy up the gravel driveway. "You, too," the man said when Frank hesitated.

"Charming," Joe said sarcastically when he and Frank were shoved into the cavernous front hall. Against each wall was a five-hundred-gallon fish tank.

"Your boss seems to like guppies," Joe commented.

"That little guppy over there is a stingray," the thug said, "and those on your right are piranha."

"Great hobby, tropical fish," Frank said.

"I find that fish are so gracefully violent," Vincent Vollrath said smoothly as he strode into the entrance hall. "Very nice work, Weldon," he added, praising the hired gun.

"Weldon, is it?" Joe drew out the name.

"His name is Dean Weldon," Vollrath said. He walked right up to Joe and stood only inches from his face. "You thought it might be something else?"

"It's the light blue eyes," Joe said. "I know a guy who had eyes that color. But his name was Brian Montrose." Joe's own blue eyes bored into Dean's. "Ever hear of him?"

Dean Weldon blinked.

"No, I'm sure he hasn't," Vollrath interrupted. "But even if he has, it really doesn't make any difference. Names are simply letters we put on papers, and that will soon be all that remains of the sons of Fenton Hardy," Vollrath sneered. "And when your famous father comes looking for you, he's going to end up the same way."

"You want me to shoot them, boss?" Weldon spoke up.

"Really now, Weldon!" Vollrath sounded embarrassed. "Nothing so crude!"

"Where's Iola Morton?" Joe demanded suddenly.

Instead of answering Joe's question, Vollrath snapped his fingers. In an instant another man emerged from the living room to join Vollrath and Weldon.

"George Kulp, these are the Hardy brothers." Vollrath introduced them as if George should really be impressed. George nodded.

"You wouldn't be George Kulp, the famous Florida warehouse tycoon, would you?" Frank asked.

Kulp's eyes widened, but he didn't say anything.

"Never mind their manners, George. I want you and Dean to show our guests around the place. I realize they have very busy schedules, but I'm sure they wouldn't want to leave without first seeing at least some of my collection of exotic marine life, am I right, boys?" He smirked at the Hardys, but clearly he did not expect them to answer. "Take them out back and show them my prize specimens," Vollrath added, "and because it's so beastly hot again today I'm sure they'd like to take a little dip in the pool."

George pulled out a gun of his own, and together he and Dean gestured for Joe, then Frank, to move through the house toward the back door. Joe was not at all surprised when they had to pause a moment for Leona Max. She was coming in from the backyard. Their captors quickly shielded their guns from view.

"What are *they* doing here?" Leona asked.

Dean hesitated and George stuttered, "N-nothing, ma'am, they just wanted to see Mr. Vollrath's, ah, aquarium."

"You don't have to concern yourself, dear," Vollrath hurried over and told her. "They'll be gone soon, anyway."

"I don't understand," she said. "Are they working for you now?"

"We'll talk about it later," Vollrath told Leona Max sharply. "George, Dean, you've got your orders."

"Really, guys," Frank said as the hoods directed him and Joe across the backyard toward one of two huge swimming pools. "We forgot our suits."

"No problem." Dean snickered.

Joe noticed that only one of the pools had a diving board and ladders.

Frank nudged his brother, then pointed out at the channel leading into Biscayne Bay. "Looks like more company's coming," Frank said.

A sleek white yacht filled Joe's field of vision. It

was pulling alongside one of several docks on the bay.

"You could sail that baby around the world," George Kulp bragged. "In fact, I think that's what the boss is going to do."

"Maybe you ought to lend those guys a hand," Joe suggested, watching the boat's four-member crew scurry around. The yacht was still moving when Joe caught sight of a bear of a man, perhaps six feet eight, jumping down onto the dock. He was dressed completely in white.

"Welcome, welcome!" Vollrath shouted as he trotted across the lawn toward his visitor. "It is a pleasure to welcome you to my humble home, Mr. Orraca. Come on up. You're just in time to watch me feed the fish."

"Rex Orraca!" Frank exclaimed.

"That's right," snapped Dean, "and you two are just in time to say goodbye."

Weldon stuck the gun in Joe's back again, then pushed him through a low chain-link fence that surrounded the pool without a diving board.

"You, too!" Kulp ordered Frank.

"Sorry we don't have a plank for you to walk," Dean Weldon sneered. "Now jump!"

Joe had been concentrating on the man in the white suit. When Weldon jabbed the gun into his back, it reminded Joe that he and Frank were in trouble.

Joe surveyed the pool. The water was cloudy green, not clear blue like regular chlorinated water. Beneath the dull, rippling surface of the pool

118

something was moving. Suddenly, as Joe Hardy's eyes widened in terror, a dark gray fin broke the surface and began circling the perimeter. Then a second fin appeared.

As if on cue, the thugs dug the barrels of their guns deeper into the backs of the Hardy brothers.

"Frank!" Joe said, recoiling. "Those are sharks in that pool!"

15 Point of No Return

"You want someone to jump in a pool of sharks," Joe Hardy said, struggling against Dean Weldon's grip, "*you* jump!"

"What's going on here?" Rex Orraca asked Vincent Vollrath when the two men reached the pool. "You throw them in there, it'll clog the filter."

Frank thought Rex Orraca looked huge in his blinding white suit. And in spite of the color of his outfit, he did not look at all like one of the good guys. He had a bull neck and squinty little eyes that darted quickly from beneath a heavy, lined brow.

"I'm just having a little fun, Mr. Orraca," Vollrath protested meekly.

"Not all of us are enjoying it," Frank informed the gangster.

Orraca glanced at Frank and Joe. "These the ones looking for the girl?" Orraca asked.

"Yes, sir," Vollrath admitted.

"You know who they are," Orraca continued, "yet you have repeatedly ignored my orders." Frank noticed it gave Orraca pleasure to watch Vollrath squirm.

"We didn't ignore your orders," replied Vollrath.

"They were supposed to be stopped before they ever got here," Orraca growled. "What happened?"

"The boys must have lost them out on the road," Vollrath whined.

"Twice is once too often," Orraca stated. "If I remember correctly," he continued, "my orders were that they were not even to reach the Florida border."

"We warned them," George Kulp chimed in.

"The orders were to *stop* them!" Orraca's eyes locked onto Vollrath.

Beads of perspiration broke out on Vollrath's forehead. "I told the men—"

"No more of your whimpering excuses," Orraca said coldly. "What about the exterminators? Did you at least take care of that like I told you to?"

"Yes, sir, of course." Vollrath was trembling now. "The fumigation site's all set up. I told the exterminators we'd call them when we're ready."

"We don't want any witnesses. I think we can manage very well without the exterminators," Orraca said, looking past the brothers. "After all, I'm not exactly untrained when it comes to getting rid of troublesome pests. Now, let's take the Hardys over to the warehouse."

Vollrath snapped his fingers. Dean and George jerked Frank and Joe away from the hungry sharks and onto the yacht.

"Put them on my boat," Orraca barked. "And tie them up."

"Vincent!" Leona Max called from the patio. Frank noticed she had been watching Vollrath's confrontation with Orraca. "There's a call for you. It's Russell Murray."

"I'll call him later!" Vollrath hollered shrilly, his voice breaking. "We've got to run up to Miami."

"Cut the small talk!" Orraca called from the heavily varnished deck of his yacht, the *Viper*.

"Nice name for a pleasure craft," Frank said dryly as Weldon and Kulp bound the brothers hand and foot in a small cabin in the *Viper*'s bow.

"This is not my idea of a Florida vacation," Joe responded.

"You realize where they're taking us," Frank said.

"Not exactly," Joe answered, "but I don't think it's any place I'd like to go."

"Remember what you found out for Dad from the phone company?"

"That's right!" Joe exclaimed. "The calls to a warehouse in Miami. Owned by George Kulp!"

"The warehouse was in his name, anyway," Frank said. "I have a feeling we're going to see that warehouse firsthand, unless we can get out of these ropes." He struggled with the bindings at his wrists. Just as he felt them slacken, someone started down the steps. Although Frank was sure he could slip one hand free, he kept his wrists together.

"Dean knows his knots," Joe said admiringly.

"I do at that," Dean Weldon said as he stepped into the cabin, holding his gun. "But it's always nice to be appreciated for one's talents."

"Like that talent you have for slashing tires," Frank guessed. "I take it you were the one who vandalized our van at that restaurant back in North Carolina."

"Nah," Dean replied, "that was some of George's work. If I had been there, we'd have run you off the highway, preferably off a bridge."

"The last two gangsters who tried that are cooling their heels in the Miami city jail," Joe said.

"What are you talking about?" Weldon grabbed Joe by his shirt and shook him.

"Do the names Russell Murray and Keith Oates mean anything to you?" Frank interrupted quickly.

"You're lying!" Dean spat. "I heard Leona Max say Russell was on the phone right before we left."

"Sure," Joe agreed. "He probably wants your fearless leader to hire a lawyer for him."

"Bring 'em up!" Vollrath called from the deck.

"You'd better hope your buddies Russell and Keith don't know where they're taking us," Frank warned Dean, "because after they've confessed to save their own skins, you'll be needing some legal aid yourself."

"The guy who's really got to worry," Joe persisted, "is the one who actually pulled off Iola

Morton's kidnapping, the guy named Brian Montrose."

Joe watched knowingly as a dark cloud of fear moved into Dean Weldon's pale blue eyes.

"Kidnapping is a very serious crime," Frank added.

"Bring them up!" Vollrath shouted down again.

"Let's go!" Weldon said, pulling himself together.

"You going to carry us?" Frank asked Dean.

Dean uttered something under his breath and untied the Hardys' feet.

"Where *is* Brian Montrose?" Joe persisted as he was pushed up on deck.

"Yes, Brian." Vollrath chuckled as he spoke to Dean. "Where are you, anyway?"

"Put the Hardys inside the warehouse," Orraca snapped from the bridge, "and make sure they're locked in."

It looked to Frank as if the yacht was docked at Miami's waterfront, next to what was a very strange sight. The older Hardy found himself staring at a giant tent made up of a patchwork of large green tarps. Because of its size and shape, the tent appeared big enough to cover a two-story building.

Frank nudged Joe and gestured toward the sign on a chain-link fence. Parking for Warehouse Systems Only, it read.

Joe nodded but could not take his eyes off the green-draped building. "It looks like a circus tent," Joe mused.

"This isn't going to be any circus," George Kulp

124

said. "That's a fumigation tent. We've got bugs in our warehouse."

"In a few minutes that tent will be filled with methyl bromide," Dean added gleefully. He pointed to a pair of scarred metal cylinders. Frank noticed that the cylinder valves were connected by a copper T, the long end of which ran under the tent flap and through a doorway into the warehouse. "Once we close up all the doors and windows, we make sure the tent is snug against the ground with these things." He held up a thin, yard-long canvas bag.

"It's too big to be a hot dog," Joe commented.

"It's a sand snake," George explained patiently. "They hold the canvas on the ground so not one little bit of gas can leak out."

"In ten minutes or less it kills anything that moves." Vollrath smirked. "But don't take my word for it," he added as he ushered the Hardys inside.

"Something's fishy in here," Joe said, sniffing the air.

"Very funny," Vollrath said without laughing. "This used to be a fish-processing facility."

"What do you use it for now?" Frank asked.

"A little of this, a little of that," the man replied.

"A little smuggling maybe?" Joe asked. The storeroom, he saw, was filled with packing crates and cartons. Many bore Oriental markings.

Vollrath ignored Joe's question. "In here," he ordered. He unlocked a padlock, then pulled open the heavy insulated door to what had once been a walk-in freezer.

125

Frank and Joe were shoved roughly into the pitch-black room. The door slammed behind them.

"Let me untie your hands," Joe said quickly. Suddenly he heard a faint gasp echo behind him. "Iola?" he whispered.

"I knew you'd find me!" a female voice cried. Someone ran into Joe, sending them both falling back onto the floor, which was covered with musty sawdust. "You guys are such great detectives! I'm so proud of you both!"

"Iola! It's really you!" Joe cried.

"Of course it's really me." She laughed, hugging the Hardys, tears of joy and exhaustion running down her cheeks. "I knew you'd find me. Did I do a good job, leaving all those clues?"

"You did just fine," Joe assured her. He hugged her again, squeezing her until she gasped. "I'm so glad to see you. Are you all right?"

"They've had me locked in here for what seems like *weeks*," Iola explained breathlessly. "There was this guy who dropped off one fast-food meal a day," she added. "I'm really tired of hamburgers and fries."

Iola pressed the little flashlight that was on her key ring into Joe's hand.

"The battery's about shot," she went on, "so most of the time I've been in total darkness." She gave Joe another hug. "I'm just so glad I have someone to talk to!"

"We want to hear all about it," Frank told Iola, "just as soon as we get out of here."

"Then let's go," she said wearily. "I don't know if

126

I can stand much more of this darkness. I'm so glad you found me so quickly. I knew you'd rescue me."

"Well . . ." Joe began.

"We found you as soon as we could," Frank explained. "Joe actually had the address to this place from the phone company. We just didn't put it all together until Vollrath caught us."

"Caught you?" Iola said. "Aren't you here to rescue me?"

"Yes and no," Frank mumbled.

"First," Joe said apologetically, "we've got to find a way out of here. And fast!"

Frank pounded on the door, then felt around the edges. "It's locked."

"We'd better do something," Joe said. "They're going to turn on the gas any minute."

"Gas!" Iola shrieked. Her knees began to buckle, and Joe had to put his arm around her waist to steady her. He knew she couldn't take much more.

While Joe explained their predicament, Frank, using the little remaining light from Iola's flashlight, located a grille in the ceiling.

"That has to be where the refrigerated air came in," Frank said. "Joe, give me a boost. Maybe we can crawl out through here.

Joe left Iola leaning against the door and helped Frank up. Standing on Joe's shoulders, Frank used a car key to remove the screws that held the grille. Next he pushed hard against the machinery above. "The entire condenser, the coils, everything seems to be up here," Frank gasped.

"We've got to move it!" Joe insisted. "There's no other way out."

"I hear something," Iola said anxiously.

Frank heard a faint hissing outside their prison.

"Get down on the floor and cover your nose," Joe instructed. Iola kneeled on the floor and covered her mouth and nose with her hands.

Frank struggled under the weight of the machinery and pushed with all his might.

"It's giving. Stand back!" Frank just managed to gasp before a sudden loud crash, like an explosion, echoed through the building.

"That was the old freezing unit," Frank announced. "It fell off the roof."

Frank scrambled up through the opening in the ceiling. Breathing heavily from the ordeal, his lungs filled with the fumes pouring out of the copper tube. Seeing an opening at the other end of the vent, he quickly crawled toward it. Would he make it before the gas knocked him out?

Below, Joe heard his brother start to say something.

"Frank?" Joe called. "Are you all right?"

Joe heard the sound of coughing and choking. He also heard the hissing sound of gas grow louder. The methyl bromide! Joe thought.

"Frank?" Joe cried out, with less volume. He wanted to call again, but he could not.

"Joe?" Iola whispered, her voice fading. "What's happening?"

"Iola . . ." Joe's voice trailed off. He knew he

had to fight to keep conscious. But the gas was so powerful, and he felt so sleepy. He tried to reach up toward the opening in the ceiling. Or, he wondered, did I only *picture* myself reaching. . . . Suddenly the only thing he could picture himself doing was lying down for a nice long sleep.

16 The Gang's All Here

I must not let the gas get to me! Frank thought as he jumped down from the vent opening and staggered across the warehouse floor. His lungs screamed for air.

Something glittering on a workbench near the door caught his eye. It was a rusty fishing knife. Frank stuck it in his belt. Fighting unconsciousness, he pulled frantically on the chain that opened an overhead door. He felt his strength ebbing away.

"Come on!" he screamed at the door.

Slowly, very slowly, it began to move. A muted green light crept across the floor from outside. He gave one mighty pull. The door went halfway up. Frank crawled under the door and grabbed hold of the tent. Using the fishing knife, Frank slashed an opening in the canvas shroud.

He gulped in the fresh sea air.

There was no time to waste, though. Joe and Iola were still trapped in the freezer. He had to shut off that gas! Frank slipped out through the tarp. Swiftly he pulled the copper tube from beneath the sand snake. Then in a single motion, he filled his lungs with air and raced back inside the warehouse for Joe and Iola.

The steady breeze blowing off the ocean had revived Joe. By the time Frank reached the freezer, he saw Joe helping Iola through the open vent. Together Frank and Joe were able to lower her to safety.

In only a short time the trio was outside on the wharf, coughing and wiping watery eyes but otherwise out of danger.

"See, you *did* rescue me!" Iola said gratefully.

"We'd better rest a minute," Frank advised. "We inhaled an awful lot of that stuff."

Joe nodded in agreement. "Any sign of Orraca's boat?" he asked.

"They're gone, probably back to Vollrath's," Frank replied, "and we're going after them."

"Alone?" Iola asked.

"No," said Frank. "I'll call Detective Ackers from the pay phone over there."

"Okay," Iola said, smiling. "That's a smart move, but the next question is, *how* are we going to go after them?"

"Have you ever thought about taking up exterminating for a living?" Joe asked playfully. He walked over to the "gnatmobile," a well-traveled standard

131

sedan with advertising messages painted all over the bright yellow body and a giant black insect on the roof. "Do you think it will bug the exterminators if we borrow their car?"

"This thing should really fly," Frank commented dryly.

The car was unlocked, and in moments Joe had the engine running. At the same time Frank got through to the Miami police department. "Detective Ackers will meet us at Vollrath's," Frank said, getting into the car. Joe nodded, shifted the car into gear, and started down the highway.

"How did you ever become entangled in this mess?" Frank asked Iola while the trio made their way back to Vollrath's house on Biscayne Bay.

"It's quite a story," Iola said. "Right after I was dragged out of Uncle Regis's car Brian Montrose took me to Vollrath's house on Gull Island."

"Why did they kidnap you in the first place?" Joe asked.

"It was Montrose's idea," Iola replied. "He knew I'd seen him at the marina the day Uncle Regis's dock was destroyed. Montrose was the one who did that. The next day when Daphne and I were on the beach, I saw him again up at Vollrath's house. He was helping unload some boxes with Chinese writing all over them. He saw me watching him, and he thought I could identify him."

"Had you realized it was Montrose who wrecked Uncle Regis's dock?" Frank asked.

"That's the crazy part," Iola admitted. "I didn't put the guy in the yellow boat at the marina

132

together with the yellow boat that hit the dock until I was kidnapped. When I told Vollrath that, he was furious with Montrose. Then Vollrath looked through my wallet and saw your picture, Joe. That really set him off. He started yelling at Montrose about me being a friend of Fenton Hardy's son and how Fenton Hardy was already investigating him."

"So that's why Vollrath wasn't surprised to see us at his house," Frank said.

Iola nodded and turned to Joe. "You found the picture, didn't you? A woman named Leona something came in the front door while they were arguing, so when Vollrath and Montrose went into the hall to stall her, I took your picture out of my purse and put it on the refrigerator with a magnet."

"I found it," Joe assured her, "and there's our van, right where we left it," he added, pulling onto Vollrath's street. He parked the gnatmobile behind the van. "I'm going right in the front. Why don't you circle around from the channel side, Frank. The police ought to be here any minute."

"What about me?" Iola asked.

"Guard this borrowed gnatmobile," Frank suggested.

"I will not!" she declared. "I'm going with Joe!"

"All right," Frank said. "But be careful."

Frank slipped onto the vacant lot adjacent to Vollrath's. His first goal was to reach the helicopter and disable it. This was easy enough.

The rest of his plan called for cutting off Vollrath and Orraca's escape by water. Frank scanned the lush tropical landscaping. Finally he spotted a sleek

133

silver powerboat anchored twenty yards out in the bay. Kicking off his shoes, Frank dived into the water.

Meanwhile, Joe and Iola scaled the stucco wall and made their way across the deserted front lawn to the portico. Joe was about to try the front door when an alarm siren sounded from inside the house.

"Joe, watch out!" cried Iola. George Kulp was coming at him from the side of the house.

Kulp took a swing at Joe. Joe faked, then put him on the deck with a stunning right to George's jaw. The front door opened, and Dean Weldon raced out.

"You!" he cried. He reached out to grab Iola, but she pulled her arm away and ran into the house past the stunned goon.

Dean lashed out, but Joe glanced a fist off Dean's ear, then pushed past him and followed after Iola.

"What *is* going on around here?" Leona Max demanded as first Iola, then Joe, and finally Dean, leaped over the chaise longue on the patio where she was sunbathing. "Have you all gone mad?"

Joe saw the *Viper* tied to Vollrath's dock. He caught a glimpse of the two gangsters on the aft deck. They were seated at a table under a bright red awning.

Orraca looked up and saw Joe. "What is it now? How'd he escape?"

"Never mind that, my men will take care of him," Vollrath said.

"That's what you said before!" Orraca yelled angrily.

Joe had landed hard on his ankle when he hurdled Leona Max. The pain slowed his speed momentarily, just enough so that Dean was able to grab his arm. Gritting his teeth, Joe vaulted the fence around the shark pool, carrying Dean with him.

"That's him! That's Brian Montrose!" Iola cried as she caught up to Joe and Dean. A swift kick by Iola in the small of Weldon-Montrose's back, and he dropped to the pool's cement apron.

"Bye-bye, Brian!" Iola said, and rolled her former kidnapper into the water.

"Help!" Dean called out.

"Help yourself!" Iola hurled back at him.

"Iola!" Joe said, reaching for Dean's outstretched hand. "There are sharks in this pool!"

Joe helped Dean out of the pool, checking momentarily to see what the men on the boat were doing. It was clear to Joe that Orraca was flying into a rage.

"You will pay for this fiasco!" he snarled at Vincent Vollrath.

"Look out!" Joe warned Iola when Orraca reached inside his spotless white suit coat. The 9-mm Beretta glinted menacingly in the bright Florida sunshine. He started down the stairs leading to the yacht's main deck. Vollrath was right behind him.

Suddenly Joe's attention turned to the sound of a racing engine, running full force.

135

"It's Frank!" Joe shouted. He pointed out toward Biscayne Bay to a fast-moving silver powerboat racing toward Vollrath's dock.

Frank waved, a huge grin on his face. In the next instant he leaped out of the boat into the bay.

"Stay under!" Joe yelled at Frank when Orraca turned the lethal weapon in an arc out over the water. Joe hollered again. "Orraca's got a gun!"

Joe jumped as Orraca squeezed off a shot. At the same instant he saw Frank's head go under the surface. The speedboat continued on its deadly course.

"Frank!" Joe's voice was drowned out by Vollrath's.

"Jump!" Vollrath shouted hysterically at the same moment the powerful boat crashed into the bay side of Orraca's *Viper*. The force of the impact was so great, the bow of the powerboat nearly sliced through both sides of the luxury vessel.

"You idiot!" Orraca shouted as he was knocked to the deck.

Orraca tried to shout another order, but Joe was relieved to hear the command muted by the sound of police sirens.

Dean struggled suddenly, trying to break out of Joe's firm grasp. Iola put a stop to it by stamping hard on his foot.

"Give it up, Orraca!" Joe demanded. Seeing police swarm over the property, Orraca threw his weapon into the channel and raised his hands.

"There's one overboard," Joe told Detective Ackers, who ran up to Joe, asking him what had happened. "Vincent Vollrath jumped off the yacht."

"And a good thing he did," Detective Ackers noted. "That boat is sinking."

"Will someone please tell me what's going on?" Leona Max asked indignantly. She had left her lounge chair and had joined Joe, Iola, and Detective Ackers near the pool. "Vincent promised me a few restful days on the Atlantic."

"I assure you," Detective Ackers told Leona Max, "you will find it very quiet down at police headquarters. You're under arrest for extortion, smuggling, and kidnapping."

The detective snapped handcuffs on her as one of his officers took Dean Weldon into custody.

"Where's Frank?" Joe called, scanning the bay.

"There he is!" Iola cried. She pointed to splashing water on the other side of the *Viper*. Joe was alarmed as he watched Frank struggling with Vincent Vollrath. Vollrath landed a hard right to Frank's chin, stunning him.

"Hang on!" Joe called, slipping off his shoes.

"He went under!" Iola cried, watching in horror as Frank slipped from view.

Joe raced to the water's edge and scanned the surface. He saw Vincent Vollrath swimming out into the bay, but where was Frank? Had Vollrath's punch knocked him out? Fear shot through Joe as he realized Frank hadn't resurfaced. If he didn't act fast, his brother would drown!

17 Surf and Sand

Joe Hardy dived into Biscayne Bay. With powerful strokes, he swam around the sinking yacht in the direction of the spot where he had last seen Frank.

Breaking the surface, he looked frantically about him.

"Joe," came Frank's voice. He sounded groggy.

Following the direction of the sound, Joe looked toward the yacht's stern. Frank was hanging on to the rudder, coughing up water.

"Don't let go!" Joe yelled, and began swimming over to his brother.

"Did you catch Vollrath?" Frank wanted to know as soon as Joe reached his side.

"We'll get him," Joe assured him.

"I'm fine, really. Which way did he go?"

"Help!" Joe stopped to listen. "Help me, I'm drowning!"

"There he is!" Frank pointed.

Joe looked out across the bay. Vincent Vollrath appeared to be going down for the third time. He was waving his arms desperately.

"Let's get him," Joe said determinedly. "I want to make sure he stands trial for kidnapping Iola."

Swimming quickly to the gangster in distress, Joe pulled the drowning hood up out of the water.

"Admit it!" Joe demanded. "Admit you kidnapped Iola Morton."

"Never," Vollrath gasped.

"Okay, Frank," Joe said, his voice steely with determination, "we've got better things to do."

Joe began swimming away.

"You can't leave me here!" Vollrath insisted.

"Did you kidnap Iola Morton?" Joe persisted.

"I did it." He gurgled. "I mean, I didn't kidnap her to begin with. That idiot Weldon took her."

"You could have let her go," Joe said.

"No, I couldn't! She saw all of us," he said.

"So you admit you kidnapped her," Joe replied.

"All right! I admit it!" Vollrath conceded. "Now get me out of here."

The confession obtained, Joe swam back to shore with Vollrath in tow. Frank swam ahead, and Detective Ackers helped him out of the water. When Joe arrived with Vollrath, Frank grabbed him and helped Ackers slip on the handcuffs.

"Vincent Vollrath, you're under arrest!" said Detective Ackers. The words were music to Joe's ears.

Twenty-four hours later, after a good night's rest in Miami, the brothers and Iola drove back across Alligator Alley to Gull Island. Joe drove the last leg. The hot Florida sun was straight overhead when he crossed over to Gull Island.

"What's Neil Jadwin doing at the Royal Palms?" Joe asked suspiciously as he pulled the van up to the motel. Jadwin was just leaving the office.

"Do you recognize that man?" Frank asked Iola.

"I've never seen him before in my life," she replied. "Is he one of the bad guys?"

"We don't think so," Joe admitted, "but as I told you, I found your watch in his cottage."

Jadwin hesitated when he recognized Frank. The Hardys jumped quickly out of the van.

"Welcome back," Jadwin said, and smiled weakly.

Joe and Frank exchanged questioning glances, then broke into broad smiles of their own when Fenton Hardy stepped out of the motel office.

"Good work!" Mr. Hardy said, greeting his sons.

"Dad!" Frank and Joe said in unison.

"Iola!" Daphne screamed. She rushed past the others, letting the screen door slam. "Are you all right?"

"My tan's starting to fade," Iola joked as she got down out of the van.

"If it is," Uncle Regis pointed out, "you've still got a little time to work on it before you go back."

140

"Where's Chet?" Iola asked. "I want to see my favorite brother."

"Iola!" Chet cried, running out of the office. He grabbed her in a big bear hug and spun her around. "Am I glad to see you! Are you all right? They didn't hurt you, did they? Because if they did . . ."

"Chet, the only one who's hurting me is you," Iola said, hugging her brother. "You're squeezing me so tight that I can't breathe!"

Everyone laughed, and Chet released his sister long enough for her to catch her breath.

"Is everyone okay?" Uncle Regis asked impatiently.

"My sons and Iola appear to be just fine," Fenton Hardy assured him, "but Rex Orraca, Vincent Vollrath, and the rest of their gang certainly can't say the same thing."

"When did you get the news?" Joe asked.

"Chet phoned," Mr. Hardy said. "He told us you'd called from Miami last night."

Neil Jadwin spoke up from the edge of the crowd. "I know you think I've broken the law, but the truth is we were on the same side."

"How's that?" Frank asked skeptically.

"Neil's an insurance investigator," Mr. Hardy explained. "Because there were so many claims all of a sudden from policy holders on Gull Island, several of the insurance companies hired Mr. Jadwin to find out what was going on."

"It was my first case," Jadwin admitted sheepishly. "I guess I didn't do a very good job. And I really messed up when I held on to Miss Morton's wristwatch. I'm glad Joe found it, even if he had to break into my house to do it."

"I threw it on the ground when Montrose grabbed me," Iola explained. "I knew Joe would recognize it."

"We know you weren't the one who kidnapped Iola," Joe told the embarrassed young investigator, "because Dean Weldon, alias Brian Montrose, confessed. He used Daphne to lure Iola out to the beach, then stole your rental car so he could commit the crime."

"If you'd reported the car stolen," Frank pointed out, "we wouldn't have wasted so much time trying to figure out what you were up to."

"I know that now," Jadwin conceded. "If I ever have the opportunity of making it up to you in some way, don't hesitate to ask me."

Chet turned to his sister, concern in his eyes. "Didn't those thugs feed you? You look as if you could float away. We'd better get some good food into you—and fast."

"That sounds like a great idea," Uncle Regis said. "Let's drive up to Bud's for a victory lunch, and the boys can tell us how they captured Vollrath."

"The food's a little greasy," Chet conceded, "but it is some of the *best* greasy food I've ever eaten."

"And my brother should know," Iola commented.

Neil Jadwin excused himself to go back to his cottage and pack.

"Good luck," Joe said, and Frank added his best

wishes as well. Jadwin waved, then hopped in his car and drove away.

"Let's have less talk and more food," Chet demanded, shepherding the group into the van. "It's time to celebrate!" Chet helped Iola into the front seat, then got in the driver's side. "Since you guys are probably exhausted from all this sleuthing, I'll even drive us into town."

The van arrived quickly at Bud's Diner. The group piled out and headed inside. Bud and Arnetta pulled several chairs up to one of the booths, and the group happily sat down. Fifteen minutes later Arnetta brought over a tray overflowing with hamburgers and steak sandwiches.

"The police searched Vollrath's warehouse," Mr. Hardy told his sons. "As you suspected, the place was filled with stolen replacement parts. The state police raided his house here on Gull Island as well. They found that box of smuggled electronic parts right where Joe said it was. Orraca was trying to expand his operation into south Florida. He cut a deal with Vollrath to use his warehouse."

"Do you think they'll get out on some kind of a plea bargain?" Iola asked.

"Not likely," Fenton Hardy speculated. "I spoke with the prosecutor, and they've got enough evidence to put the whole gang away for a long time."

"I think Keith Oates and Russell Murray will cooperate with the prosecutors," Frank added. "Detective Ackers said Murray admitted Vollrath ordered him and Kulp to follow us down from

143

Bayport. He had been sent up to follow Dad until they kidnapped Iola."

"Vollrath was getting his orders from Orraca," Fenton Hardy put in. "Orraca knew I was hunting for him, even before I did. So he sent Vollrath's men to slow us down."

"So they were after you fellows," Uncle Regis said, "but what was the reason for the rest of the vandalism here on the island?"

"Vollrath wanted to buy up Gull Island," Frank explained, as he cut into his steak. "He'd heard through his gangland connections that Rex Orraca wanted to move his entire operation to Florida. What could be better than owning a sleepy little island off Florida's west coast?"

"So he sent out his boys to cause a few accidents," Joe continued. "Oates was responsible for stealing the palm trees and smashing our window."

"Some of it could have put Regis out of business, though," Fenton Hardy commented. "Sam Radley spoke with officials at the motel's reservation booking service, who admitted one of Orraca's Chicago enforcers leaned on them to cancel Regis's account. Sam's cleared up that end of the case."

"Vollrath was trying to give the residents a good reason to sell out," Joe concluded. "Like the phony state inspector. That was Murray."

"What about Leona?" Daphne asked. "Did they put that witch in jail, too?"

"Don't be surprised if Leona Max turns out to be the state's star witness against Vollrath," Frank said.

"That's right," said Joe. "It turns out she didn't know anything about Vollrath's criminal connections. She simply thought she'd hooked up with a rich guy who wanted to marry her and make a whole new fortune developing Gull Island. He told her they'd live happily ever after on their own private island."

"She's still got her vacant lot on Pelican Lane," Arnetta reminded them as she brought a second plate of food to the table, much to Chet's delight. "She can always pitch a tent."

"By the way, Frank," Fenton asked, "who's boat did you demolish when you sank Orraca's yacht?"

"I wasn't sure when I borrowed it," he said, smiling, "but it turned out to be Vollrath's. Since he was responsible for the bomb that destroyed Uncle Regis's cabin cruiser, it helps balance the scales of justice."

"What I still don't know," Joe said, turning to Iola, "is how you ever managed to mail that postcard to Chet."

"That's right," Frank agreed. "If you hadn't left us that trail of clues, we might still be sitting around here wondering where to start."

"Let's see," Iola said. "I picked up the postcard at Vollrath's. Vollrath told Montrose to keep me out of sight. He took me up to an office on the second floor. I kicked him in the shin, and he shoved me into the desk chair. He told me if I moved, I'd be sorry. I told him *he* was the one who was going to be sorry. He was really upset. He kept saying, 'What else could I do?' and then he said he had to get rid of the stolen car and he left."

"Weren't you scared to death?" Chet asked, swallowing the last piece of his second hamburger.

"I was more angry than scared," Iola said. "Daphne and I had been waiting weeks for this vacation. I sure didn't want to spend it being kidnapped."

"That's right," Daphne agreed.

"Anyway," Iola continued, "I was in that office, so I looked around and I saw this stack of postcards of the Miami waterfront. I stuck one in the pocket of my shorts. Then I saw there were stamps on the desk, so I took one of those, too, and a pen."

"That was pretty slick," Joe said admiringly, "but how did you ever mail it?"

"They flew me over to Miami in Vollrath's helicopter," Iola continued. "They untied me when they locked me in the warehouse freezer, and a couple times a day a man would let me use the facilities in the warehouse office. That's when I mailed the card."

"Let me guess," Chet said. "You befriended this guy, and he mailed the card for you."

"No," Iola said, "I simply dropped the card into the wire out basket on the warehouse foreman's desk. The gang mailed it!"

"Clever!" Joe whistled.

"Thank you, thank you." Iola smiled and bowed from her seat. "Now, I came down here to lie on

146

the beach, and that's exactly what I'm going to do!"

"Sounds good to me," Joe agreed. "We have a few days left in our spring break. We might as well take advantage of them."

"You know, it *will* be relaxing just to lie around under the palm trees," Frank said.

"And maybe get up every hour or so," Joe said, "and take a dip in the gulf."

"Let's agree that nothing will interrupt the rest of this vacation," Daphne suggested.

"Good luck," Chet said, winking at the Hardys.

"Why do you say that?" Frank wanted to know.

"You know you two can't just lie around and do nothing for several days," Chet said. "Besides, while you were away, Uncle Regis told me a legend about a sunken galleon on that reef off the south shore."

"What legend?" Joe wanted to know.

"Just some story about missing gold doubloons," Uncle Regis said, chuckling.

"Now, Joe!" Iola interrupted, slipping on the red-framed mirrored glasses she'd gotten especially for the bright Florida sun. "What about the beach?"

"Sounds great," Frank said. "Maybe some scuba diving would be fun, too. I can't wait to check out that reef."

"Yeah," Joe agreed. "It's probably full of ships."

"Think about all the tropical fish we'll find," Frank added.

"And sunken treasure," Chet said.

Daphne and Iola exchanged glances. Iola shrugged. She'd seen that gleam in Joe's eye too many times. "All right," she said, "I know when I'm beat. When do we start?"

THE HARDY BOYS® SERIES By Franklin W. Dixon

NANCY DREW® MYSTERY STORIES By Carolyn Keene

MEET THE *NEW* BOBBSEY TWINS™

THE BOBBSEY TWINS ARE BACK
AND BETTER THAN EVER!

When older twins Nan and Bert and younger twins Freddie and Flossie get into mischief, there's no end to the mystery and adventure.

Join the Bobbsey twins as they track down clues, escape danger, and unravel mysteries in these brand-new, fun-filled stories.

The *New* Bobbsey Twins:

__ #1	The Secret of Jungle Park	62651	$2.95
__ #2	The Case of the Runaway Money	62652	$2.95
__ #3	The Clue That Flew Away	62653	$2.95
__ #4	The Secret in the Sand Castle	62654	$2.95
__ #5	The Case of the Close Encounter	62656	$2.95
__ #6	Mystery on the Mississippi	62657	$2.95
__ #7	Trouble in Toyland	62658	$2.95
__ #8	The Secret of the Stolen Puppies	62659	$2.95
__ #9	The Clue In The Classroom	63072	$2.95
__ #10	The Chocolate-Covered Clue	63073	$2.95
__ #11	The Case of the Crooked Contest	63074	$2.95
__ #12	The Secret Of The Sunken Treasure	63075	$2.95
__ #13	The Case Of The Crying Clown	55501	$2.95
__ #14	The Mystery Of The Missing Mummy	67595	$2.95
__ #15	The Secret of the Stolen Clue	67596	$2.95
__ #16	The Case of the Missing Dinosaur	67597	$2.95
__ #17	The Case at Creepy Castle	69289	$2.95
__ #18	The Secret at Sleepaway Camp	69290	$2.95
__ #19	The Show and Tell Mystery	69291	$2.95
__ #20	The Weird Science Mystery	69292	$2.95
__ #21	The Great Skate Mystery	69293	$2.95
__ #22	The Super-Duper Cookie Caper	69294	$2.95
__ #23	The Monster Mouse Mystery	69295	$2.95
__ #24	The Case of the Goofy Game Show	69296	$2.95
__ #25	The Case of the Crazy Collections	73037	$2.95
__ #26	The Clue at Casper Creek	73038	$2.99
__ #27	The Big Pig Puzzle	73039	$2.99

__ #28 The Case of the Vanishing Video
73040-1 $2.99

__ #29 The Case of the Tricky Trickster
73041-X $2.99

MINSTREL® BOOKS